GHOSTS

ALSO BY CURDELLA FORBES

Fiction for Young People
Flying with Icarus

Adult Fiction
Songs of Silence
A Permanent Freedom

Non-Fiction
From Nation to Diaspora: Samuel Selvon, George Lamming and the Cultural Performance of Gender

CURDELLA FORBES

GHOSTS

A MEMOIR

In memory of my brother,
Anthony Jehudi Forbes (Tony),
October 18, 1958 – July 31, 2000

PEEPAL TREE

First published in Great Britain in 2012
Peepal Tree Press Ltd
17 King's Avenue
Leeds LS6 1QS
England

ISBN13: 9781845232009

Supported by
ARTS COUNCIL
ENGLAND

CONTENTS

ROOT

My family was born with a wound. Whether it was a private wound, peculiar to us and our generations, or the wound of history, or Adam's wound, the wound of the world, I do not know. My father's family was Morris, and my mother's Pointy. We were born on the Caribbean island of Jacaranda, and though we travelled a great deal and were restless, often even living in other parts of the world, this was where we grew up and this was where, in a manner of speaking, we lived for all of our lives. Our country was colonized by the English for centuries, and so we had these two names, Morris, Pointy, that made it sound as though we were white people, from England, or Scotland, or Ireland, or Wales, though we were black people. In the beginning, when we became curious about our names, we were told that Morris came from the Irish side, because our great great grandfather on my father's side was Irish. At the time, because we were children, and brought up in an anachronistic, back-o-time household where we knew nothing about sexual intercourse except that sometimes young couples were found giggling in corners, and sometimes adults sent us away, out of hearing or out of the room, so that they could whisper, it did not occur to us to wonder how my great great grandfather came to be an Irishman, or whether someone, a woman, a girl, had been taken advantage of, which was how in those days in such remote districts as ours, our people spoke about the act of rape.

Pointy, we were told, though I don't know by whom, came from the French side, a corruption of Ponteau, a name meaning 'bridge', after a French Huguenot who escaped to the island in the seventeenth century and impregnated a wandering slave woman who became our ancestor.

A French and an Irish side, divided by a channel of water, for which a bridge was needed for crossing over.

The only person I ever heard speak about the African side, the side that showed in our skins and our faces, was our mother. She did not speak of this side as though it was a part of our name. Not because she was ashamed, but because she took it for granted that we were black, and to show this, no name was necessary. To be a person, my mother said, was just to be. You asked questions about who you were, only when you were unsure. But we lived above the banks of a river in a behind-God-back district in a far far country, and every morning when the mists rose above the water, my mother saw processions of slave women with washpans on their heads, passing along the riverbank on their way to somewhere that caused them to sing – whether in repudiation or celebration, my mother could not tell, because the murmur of their voices was one with the sound of the river water washing over the stones. She told us about these daily sightings, and I thought these women whom she saw might be our long ago relatives, since other generations of us had lived there before. But so had the generations of the rest of the district, so who was to say? Our family was so huge and sprawling, and as children growing up we were so happy, our lives so full (of adventure, of quarrelling, of dreaming, of laughing, of chaos), that we never worried about these things; limbs missing from family trees were neither things we cared about, nor wounds that we even knew we had.

My aunt had a vague memory that we had some Indian blood, which has left no mark except in the wideness of the kinks in our hair, which could as well have been on account of the Irish. Our Indian forbear, she said, was a coolie-royal boy (a boy of mixed Indian and African blood, which in our country was royalty, not disgrace, not dougla) who turned up at the gate of our great grandmother on the Morris side when she was barely sixteen, and she loved him so fiercely and so well because of the glow in the wide black curls of his hair, that she walked out of her father's gate with her clothes tied up in one bundle, took his hand in hers and left her district forever, to settle with him, her perfect prince, in the district that became our home. But her father never spoke to her again, and wrote in his will that she was to get only a Willix penny, 'on account of inappropriate behaviour'. People in the district and everywhere I have travelled, say that the slant in my eyes is Chinese, but we have no knowledge of this, and moreover we have seen Africans with slanted eyes.

It is easy to make much of these things, but they are not the real story of our wound. I mention them only to give a little background about us. Our wound was not a wound we knew about from the beginning. We knew it was there only because of the strange deformities it produced in us: double limbs, replicated organs, superstitions, dreams, uncanny affections, genius, peculiar retardations, quarrels, guilt, an abiding desire to rescue and be rescued, and the most implacable tendency to obsession. The brief, half-told story that follows in these pages is the story of how these wounds manifested in one small node, in one capsule of time, in the lives of the elder four of us, over a period of years. You could say it is the story of how my brother died, and when, and where, and why, and the story of the various ways in which, because of this, all of us died, and lived.

Because we lived in a district that was small and isolated, yet constantly open to global traffic in any number of ways (journeys – to and fro –, internets, remittances, telephones, cables, books, an obsession with looking out over mountains to where there was another sea) a great many rumours circulated about me and my siblings, and it was said that our family was mad. Truth to tell, I believe my family is mad. But this rumour was not the story that I wanted our grandchildren and grandnieces and grandnephews to hear, when their time came to ask the questions they would inevitably ask about the family and its scars. So I said to my siblings, let us make an album, a family album telling our part in what happened to our brother, and I will put it together for our children.

I gave my word that I would play no part except the part of putting it together, because I knew I did not have their trust. My sister Beatrice spoke for the others when she said my lying tongue would get in the way of everybody's truth. I have made my living as a writer, and so my siblings have never trusted me. When I close a book and later reopen it, I find that the words have slipped out of joint, out of their assigned places, as if print is written in water. And I find myself mending the story, trying to fix it in its place. A futile and heartsick undertaking, not to mention a perverse one, since a story already deformed is incapable of staying in its place, and will fight very hard to lead you by the nose, and it will win, always it will win, once I try to tamper, because the taint in the story that made it slip out of joint in the first place was not in the story but in me. If you gave me a thousand and one days, it would still be marred forever.

So I tried very hard to keep out of this one, which is a memoir, in which the facts must have their day, a family memoir, in which each of us must have room to speak. Still, only three of my siblings were willing to take the risk of handing over their stories to me, even for posterity's sake. This, and the family wound, which still longs to shield itself, is the reason this album is a fragment, a brief stitching of fragments torn from a claw, the claw of memory, of forgetting.

I humbly thank my sister Beatrice and my sister Evangeline for their trust in me. Their stories are here faithfully set down, as they gave them to me. I thank also my mother Seraphine for the family histories she told us on the front step, shelling peas, or in the kitchen, stirring pone. These histories helped me to stitch together the parts that happened before I was born.

I pay homage to my brother Pete, from whose diaries the story of his relationship with our cousin Tramadol is pieced together. For the most part I have set down his exact narrative as set out in the diaries. It is only at the end, where I have imagined Tram's long struggle with the change of life, based on her telephone conversations with Beatrice, that I have allowed my own words to intervene. The decision to use Pete's diaries, when he was not there to give us permission, was a very hard one indeed, but I think it was the right decision because it reveals the beauty of my brother and the integrity of my cousin, which are contrary to the rumours circulating. I think Pete wanted me to do this, because of the way he left the diaries, in the secret compartment of the strong box to which, in his will, he left me the key.

I thank especially my elder sister Evangeline, who did not write her story herself but gave me permission to write it for her. It is characteristic of the grace of this sister, whom we call the seer, that she did not ask to see the script before I placed it in the album. It is also characteristic that in this album she takes up more space than everyone else, even when she is self-effacing, as she always, truly, is. The humblest ones loom largest in our eyes. I tell myself this is the reason there is more from my keyboard than from the others', this and not the fact that I may have gone overboard, chasing after the words that again unlodged themselves, when it was my turn to speak. If there is too much of me in this album, forgive.

My final word to our generations is this: I do not know how you will interpret this album. I have not tried to link it to any history except the immediate history of our private, familial, psychic wounds, but it may be that you will find other linkages, other cleavages, in the history we share with others in our country and the rest of the world. It is not for me to say. There is one thing though, a set of facts, that I discovered about our family after this album was put together, that might actually help you to make sense of it all. This I placed in the Afterword (which I have entitled 'Coda') so as not to detract from your freedom in drawing your own conclusions.

And finally. (In my country, we conclude twice, and say goodnight many times, going out the door). In the Global Museum of Printed Books, of which a branch is located in the Institute of Jacaranda at this time, there is a book of tales in which is to be found one entitled 'The Six Swans'. There were six brothers and one sister, and because of a wickedness (not theirs) over which they had no control, the brothers were changed into swans, and sent away, and could only be made human and to return again, if their sister sewed for them magic shirts, over seven years, without speaking. And this she did succeed in doing, except that before the sixth shirt could be finished, she spoke prematurely, out of necessity, and the

13

youngest brother got a shirt without a sleeve, and thus received back intact only one arm, remaining forever winged. I imagine that with one arm and one wing, this maiming and freedom on both sides, this boy, like his sister who invented without speaking, and then spoke and could no longer invent (she, like him, maimed and free in both instances), would always be struggling to put things back in their places, a place of perfection, to put back together flying and grounding, speech and silence, both and each together in a balance of timing as exquisite as the timing of the spheres. And yet it may be that if they are doomed to this struggle forever, never reaching fulfilment, it is because the taint is not in either of these two sets of things but in the heart inside of them, which they were given from their father, and their mother, cleaved in the middle, with ventricles carrying blood, one thicker than the other.

And it's the same thing all over, you know. Not just in our family. So don't break your heart with bad feeling. By the time you are reading this, the world will have changed beyond recognition. In my own short lifetime so much has happened. We now have computers cleaning our houses and taking our children to school, piloting driverless cars. In another twenty-four months, China and the USA are thinking, construction will begin on their joint-colony on the moon. We have killed out AIDS (though not the common cold; a cure for that eludes us, just to curb our hubris). Now blind people can see as well as seeing-eyed people, and even in Jacaranda, thanks to the Global Electrical Grid, there are some children who don't know what an electricity pole looks like since the cities have gone wireless. By the time you are reading this, China might have sunk into the sea and Trinidad become the new super-power. Any number can call, don't fret. But the thing that strikes you is how we still dreaming, still hungering, still hoping, still having faith, still getting fat or maaga or slim; and how we still destroying, with every move of progress we make: look how many diseases replacing AIDS; how many people hungry all the time; how much war fight; and as I put this album together I can't help wondering if any of you, my children's children, my nieces' children, my nephews' children, will be here to read it, seeing-eye or no seeing eye, if the sea don't stop caving in on us from greenhouse gas or that big hole in the ozone don't stop turning our skin blue. For no matter what change, the heart don't change. And is out of heart all these things come, one ventricle thicker than the other.

But your grand-aunt, or your ancestor, Evangeline, says we live by God's grace.

May you by grace be holding in your hands this flutter of pieces, this frazzle of flight, after we done put it away.

I

THE CHANGE OF LIFE

On October 24, 2014, Tramadol Pointy suddenly became beautiful. That is to say, after years (two to be exact) of watching, heartbroken, the easy-walking lilt of girls with wire waists, dutchpot derrières and upstanding, ripe-naseberry breasts, girls bright-eyed and flush with the know-ingness of their beauty and irresistibly tinkling feet, Tramadol looked into the suddenly shining mirror on her wall and saw in her own eyes and lips grown violet and lush with promise, her pert breasts and come-out-of-nowhere hips rounding like plump pears above now impossibly long legs, something that she knew would change the shape the world had taken up to that present time. Beyond the discomfiture of thirsty schoolboys clamouring at the fountain of her love, Tramadol looked into the future and saw a place of fire and ice where her feet were now set, towards a destiny that had been marked out for her, without her collaboration or will. It was as devastating as if she had looked into the mirror and found she had become a beetle.

This sudden revelation came at a price. Tramadol was my cousin. And she inherited the family curse like the rest of us. Straight after her transformation she developed three obses-sions: a deep hunger for love, that is to say, the expectation of a prince, fiercer than fire or time, who would show her the meaning and origin of the stars; a desire for faraway places, places struck deep, like newly minted coin, with desert fire or the ice of fjords, mountains of frost breaking apart the face of oceans; and, at the last, an obsession with antique timepieces, among which she numbered an hourglass full of mercury. If she had been forced to give an account of these passions, Tramadol would have denied that they had anything to do with the hold reading had on her. That is to say, even though to escape the taunts of schoolmates who mocked her for lacking breasts and hips and the bursting facial pustules that announced the onset of womanhood; scorned her for wearing shoes that her grandfather had patched with his own hands using thread that showed grey against the dark brown of the shoes; giggled when she missed so many days at school that the English mistress scarcely raised her head to remark, 'I see you are with us today, Inspector'; mimicked her for being unable to speak, her tongue tied with the perpetual anguish of her outsiderness – even though to escape the pain of all this, Tramadol had for many years buried herself in the cool forests of certain kinds of books, with angry deserts, ice mountains, and romances that flared between princes and princesses on cobalt seas*, she would have said her passions had nothing to do with bookish romance, but something else altogether. That something else I leave to you to discern. But be patient for the story of this love. It unfolds slowly, it going tek time.

With the coming of her beauty Tramadol raided heart closets and killed dragons. Boys at school fell like ninepins. It wasn't Tramadol's desire to slay any: her sole aim and driving thirst was to find the one man worthy of loving her, her prince of away places, her man of fire and uncareful feet, and ice. Tram was one of those girls who treated men badly because she was beautiful and she knew that made us stupid. At the same time, she behaved towards her beauty like a deprived child let loose in a toy shop; like any young girl in her position, she flirted lavishly, and with a fine and prodigal cruelty. Yet she was exceedingly vulnerable to the idea of love, and on three distinct occasions my cousin fell briefly, violently, and with a storm of tears, in love.

As each of the three would-be princes failed the test, my cousin blamed herself for setting her sights too low. The thing that you have to understood about my cousin – the thing that

---

* In our own country, Jacaranda, the sea was undecided and indeterminate – fawn as an eagle's eyes, colourless as light, as often rose pink and stained grape as it was fantasy's lapis lazuli or cobalt blue

few people knew, for very few, if any, knew her at all (even I who was closest to her, knew her less through intimacy than through the cage of a haunted imagination) – is that she gave her total allegiance to love; for her, love was the highest value, and to offer or ask less than the best from love was the worst form of apostasy. If she had been religious you could have called her a visionary. As it was, I used to think she had been born in the wrong place and time. I imagined her against a backdrop of olive groves, in ancient Greece, a votary at Aphrodite's shrine, or a virgin in calm desert tents, feeding pomegranate seeds to princes. The names that people used to call her as a heartless heartbreaker – Sketel, Boy Crazy, Man Crazy, Tek Too Much Man, Iron Front, Gi Man Bun, Tram-Car (Everybody ride pon har) – she didn't deserve, first because my cousin was very chaste, and second, because with every failure you saw in her eyes a desolation that said her grief was even greater than her suitor's. But beauty such as Tramadol's is the stuff of which legends are made, and these nicknames, denoting a gargantuan sexual appetite, served the cause of legend as well as the need of expiation (for extreme beauty has always to be atoned for).

Each time she called off an assay into a new relationship (for you couldn't call these knot-up ropes actual relationships), my cousin retreated to her room and lay on her bed for many days, not moving, staring up at the invisible ceiling above the concrete one, like a self-abnegating prophetess waiting for a sign. Nothing I did could bring her out of these trances. That is to say, sometimes, if I beat the door long and hard enough, she opened it, let me in, and went back to her speechless vigil, ignoring both my words and my silence, offered in what (vainly, with self-acknowledged hubris) I hoped was close companionship; at other times, after she let me in, she answered my questions in riddles, mystical sayings and bookish quotations that were as strong a wall as when she didn't say anything. My cousin had lived inside her own head for so long that she made up a language of her own, the kind that twins make up when they want to keep everyone else out.

Most of the time she wouldn't open the door.

During these crises my cousin again underwent strange transformations. Her face and body would pass through a series of grotesques, huge serpentine twistings that I, the only witness, never dreamed of divulging to the family. First, who would believe me? And second, they invoked in me a deep superstition, the fear that if I spoke them, the words would become flesh and either my cousin would be doomed to encounter them forever, or I too would be taken over and become forever the bodily cage of writhing lamias, higues and ancient soucouyants. I cried out in my sleep with the burden and secret of them. Sometimes, even now, as if it's happening again, I relive the terror I felt whenever in the midst of one of these seizures my mother stopped at the door to demand, 'What's going on in there? What the two of you lock up inside there doing?' They made my cousin exceedingly ugly, with the ugliness that one finds at the roots of cotton trees guarding skulls that rain has washed out from the soil, long after the graves have sunk – graves made in the old days before people were buried in concrete vaults and were instead put direct into the ground in cedar boxes. Tramadol's face had the same stark ugliness of beauty stretched to its uttermost extreme, the ghastly, naked skull of confrontation and the black roots of nether substance that sheltered it. After each terrific convulsion, her face smoothed out like a sheet of brown paper, beautiful and pure once more, the tortured limbs slowly following suit, curving sweet like the lilt of songs. I could not begin to guess what horrors, or ecstasies my cousin encountered in the grip of these dread trances.

'But what yu really want, Tram?' I asked on one of the rare occasions when she opened the door. 'Yu confuse me same as how yu confuse the yout-dem dat checking yu. Yu vex wid dis one because him don't open the door for yu, ladies before gentlemen, him catch up himself, yu run him. Yu say t'idda one too mean, yu hate man dat come to visit yu wid nutten in him hand an first ting him do is open yu fridge. Well, mi understand dat. But yu talk to him bout it, him repent, him half kill yu wid flowers an poetry an apology, the yout tun yu slave, yu seh him too conceited. If me was a woman an yout change like dat fi mi, mi heng on pon him. An what about Charlie? Granted mi nuh like di bredda, but Charlie is the gentleman's gentleman, mi see di bredda walk pon water fi yu. So what's the score?'

'Though I speak with the tongues of men and of angels,' Tram said obscurely.

'What?'

'First Corinthians 13. Hymn to love. It tell yu what is real love.'

'Tram, don't gimmi dat for yu don't even believe inna Bible. Yu hate church like how puss hate water. Yu not Evangeline. So where dis coming from?'

'Yes, but dem don't offer love,' my cousin said, by way of translation. 'Those are just trivialities. Is what they point to you must look at.'

'But Tram, not opening the door can be just upbringing, you know. First of all how many guys you know who know anything bout dem kinda ting from dem yard? And further-more, these days it so confusing – the way some o oonu woman go on, it mek man think opening door an dem kinda ting dere is anti-feminist, like thinking of the woman as the weaker vessel. Yu remember when Aunt Rita sprain her back and had to travel from Birmingham to London to catch the plane from Heathrow to come home, and she couldn't lift her suitcase in the train and the whole heap a man pass her there, none o dem offer to help?'

Tram sucked her teeth. 'Cheups. Dat nuh feminism, dat a racism. So nuh bring no white man into dis conversation. Tell mi something: dese boys dat brukking dem neck to get into mi underclothes, dem don't go to school? Dem might born a backabush, but dem go to school, dem suppose to learn something. An if dem nuh learn it, dem damn dunce so mi wussar don't want dem. Is not just the opening of the door – yu never notice how di boy always expec mi fi walk backa him? Him always a lead di way, always out in front. Is a personality defect dat.' After a silence she added in the prim voice that told you she didn't want to cry, 'It points to a certain lack of emotional intelligence.'

It was a long speech for her, exceedingly rare.

'Can a man change?'

I asked this hopelessly, because even then I knew she didn't think of me as a man. The price I paid was her confidence. Even then, I knew I would love her forever. Even if even second cousins could not marry, could not boil good soup, except in the sly proverb that said cousins sometimes did, in secret. Cousin an cousin boil good soup. Hee hee. It was the main reason my mother would tear off the door, metaphorically speaking, to get us to open up so she could see or smell what we had been doing. My mother had no idea that I was the safest person in the whole wide world to Tram, because Tram thought of me as a sister. Six feet by the time I was fourteen and my cousin thought I was a girl.

'Hog mout nuh grow long overnight.'

I understood the cryptogram. This was my cousin's way of saying, sure, a man can change, in so far as he grows into the person he is going to become, but nobody changes at the fundament. Pretty much, the apparatus you start out with is what you carry to your grave.

'But suppose what yu seeing now is di –' I struggled for a word, 'you know, di – call it then di excess – di excess dat show dat the man don't grow into him full self as yet? Like cane trash – yu know, how cane trash can cover good cane an yu haffi tear it off to see the real juicy cane underneath?'

'Boss man, if yu see a snake a-run pon top o di cane, chances are, one nest underneath there.'

'So yu nuh see no potential dat yu can work with, in any man so far?'

'Boy pickini, hear dis. I don't want no man potential. Dat is like eating air pie an breeze pudding. Yu see me offering any man my potential? Fixing up myself is my responsibility. Dem, ditto.'

I never knew anyone as exigent as Tram. Most girls – and later, women – I knew were willing to forgive a man many things. Probably most things. Even my sisters, who were strong, independent women, had forged forms of compromise they could live with. Beatrice, the fiercest of them, said

24

the one thing she could never forgive was physical abuse. 'Dat kind of man never change,' according to B. 'It in dem DNA. Psychiatrist might mask it for a while, but sooner or later it front up again, just like how the sea going come back one day an reclaim all dem dump-up land where they put house and call it city. Water find its own level. Man like that, nuh fi go near no woman, mus stay by himself.'

I agreed with B; we had grown up in a district where two well known women, married to two brothers, were constantly at the receiving end of domestic assault and battery; my mother, the district's unofficial lawyer, on occasion took it upon herself to gather posses of villagers to go and drag these men off their wives, on whom they'd be sitting wielding cricket bats and once even a knife. And when we were young together, before I got introduced to the pleasures of sexual intercourse and found that it had nothing to do with commitment, I agreed with B and Peaches that infidelity was also serious cause for concern and in certain cases would have to be fatal. I know I could not have been unfaithful to Tram, even if I had wanted to. My cousin made no exceptions, gave no quarter.

Tramadol's pronouncements on the subject of men are responsible for my bachelorhood. Either I seem to have spent my life looking for her in other women's faces, or she instilled in me such an absolute terror of falling short, that I make tracks as soon as a woman I'm involved with starts asking the kind of questions that mean she wants to 'get to know me better' – code for checking me out as potential husband material.

Tram was probably the brightest of us, but she didn't do well in school. For one thing, the crises of broken love drained her strength. But she was also convinced that you shouldn't waste time on irrelevancies, including those your parents prescribed for your own good. And so once she knew what her own destiny was, she pursued it with fierce and single-minded concentration so that her schoolwork suffered, and her tendency to retreat into the world made by words, that is to say, the words of others that made new worlds out of thin air (for she herself hardly spoke) became morbid. At intervals she could not bear to be inside a building, otherwise she became feverish, once catching pneumonia. Her only relief at such times was to take walks, over and over again, by the river that ran below my grandparents' house. Indian kale used to grow there, and she would look deeply into their roots, like someone reading runes. She read as well birds, flowers, canes, the shape of rose-apples – the little golden fruit smelling of perfume that also grew by the water – and the strange figures that whirled in the pools. She was fascinated by the upside down world under the surface of river water. For my cousin, all of these things posed parables, hieroglyphs of meaning that were the key to what the universe meant, a parallel world which was the real image of the one we saw when we opened our eyes in the morning. In all of this, Tramadol was looking for ways to recognize her prince, so when he came she would know him. (Be patient for the story of this love. It unfolds slowly, like roses in cool places).

Over the years, at various stages of hindsight, I have tried to work out why my cousin chained me so completely to herself, even though I was obviously not the prince. I think that because I was myself so ordinary, I fell profoundly in love with my cousin's way of saving herself. Tram knew that life poses itself as a riddle – that it offered more than anyone could see with the naked eye, but most people didn't know that, or if they knew, the terror of the price to be paid made them willing to settle for a little (or a great deal) less. Tram was the only person I knew who refused to compromise on the promise of life. She was going to seize it by the throat and make it give up everything it had hidden in its marrow, perversely stashed away for the violent. Here again my cousin quoted the Bible, in which she had no religious interest.

'Only the violent take it by force, boss boy,' she said in one of her rare moments, eyes glistening with a desire for the fray that I found sexually exciting. 'To go in and out without hindrance at all the gates of the Duat.' That was from the Egyptian Book of the Dead.

I didn't think of what I came to call Tram's way as possibly a form of perversity, maybe because I was too obsessed with her, with the obsession of the ordinary for the spectacular. That is to say, I didn't wonder whether what I saw in her as integrity was in fact a deep selfishness, or whether her absolute certainty about what she wanted was more accurately a profound cynicism, frightening in one so young. It was Tramadol who, constantly self tortured, asked those questions of herself, over and over again in Gordian knots like a lamia's tail, or a rolling calf's chain. My cousin was both tortured and free. I thought her brave and splendid, like the full round moon. Yet I constantly struggled with her, out of a conviction that at the centre of the world there was a bridge, called Compromise, which everyone crossed over to get to the other side, but no one could go on unless someone on the opposite bank came to meet them halfway, and then the two returned together.

In contrast, what Tram saw at the centre of the world was the lake of fire and ice, which was to be won only by many passages of death, and which, once one dipped one's body in it, would open one's eyes to reveal the one twin soul, who had also come all the way, not halfway, on this journey, and with whom one would return across the freezing, burning steppes, one's body also transformed.

Tram's vision of the right man evolved over the years, but in each permutation I recognized the boy she had longed for in our teenage years. Finally, in my struggles and remonstrances with my cousin, I came to see that what she wanted was so simple it was impossible. My cousin wanted a lover who would accept her as she was, so utterly and completely that she would never be at risk of judgement or abandonment.

I often wondered if her refusal to risk rejection was because, unlike the rest of us, Tram had no parents whom she could separate out and run to in the seething exuberant mass of our overlarge family, no one she could assure herself, at a moment's notice, belonged to her and her alone. Tram came to live with us when she was five years old, after her father, my mother's first cousin, was killed falling off a goods truck, his skull hitting the pavement with a trivial sound like a child popping a soda box. She didn't know her mother, who had left her on the hospital bed for her father to come and pick up, like the parcel of belongings that one must collect upon discharge. After that, her mother disappeared. No one knew where she went. She was a young girl, named Mia, who had lived by herself under a tree until my grandparents took her in and brought her up. My mother's cousin, Tram's father, fell in love with her and gave her the baby who was Tram, while she was still very young and had not seen life beyond the boundaries of our small district. My mother's cousin wanted to marry her, which fact drove Mia, child of the open pasture, catatonic with the terror of confinement, and so, after the baby was born, she ran. My maternal grandparents adopted their granddaughter in the matter-of-fact way of our people, and she was absorbed into the great beehive of our clan that made people say when we emerged in force for family outings, 'Heh, Barber an him tribe a-come.' My parents lived in the main yard with my mother's parents and brought up their seven children there. All my mother's siblings and their children lived nearby, within walking distance, and in a sense none of them had ever left the main yard, which still remained the place of daily gathering, after work, church and school, for themselves and their children, later their children's children, until my grandparents, the Rigel and Betelgeuse around which these satellites revolved, passed on. With twenty-six siblings, cousins, aunts, uncles, nieces and nephews milling about on an ordinary day, ours was a large and noisy yard in which children were treated with an evenhanded affection as careless as the sun's largesse. All the children belonged to all the parents and the names 'Mama' and 'Papa' got hopelessly mixed up and exchanged among the various mothers and fathers from the time we were able to talk. (When we grew a little older we distinguished between our birthparents and our uncles and aunts by saying 'Mama' and 'Papa' for our birthparents and 'Uncle Papa Dunstan' or 'Aunty Mama Mouse' for the others). Most of us flourished like wild weeds in that siege, but for Tram this democratic affection was always too thinly spread. She wanted to matter, separate and apart from our family's prodigal and indiscriminate loves. She stood aloof from the crowd of us; our company drained her, made her grow damp and feverish and unable to speak, so that my mother more than once had to treat her for lockjaw, pouring bizzi tea between her clenched teeth until my cousin's frenzied eyes rolled back to their right position in her head. But we were of an age, she and I, and because her silence and her fits fascinated me I took time to play with her, share my games; after a while, between intervals of wordless retreat, she started shadowing me, silent, big-eyed and, until sixteen, preternaturally ugly, and so we became friends, I her slave.

Perhaps my cousin's life might have been less tragic if her name had been different. In a place where names often had meaning based on their sound (in the same way as laughter or cries), her father heard the name Tramadol on television and thought it musical. But it was a name for pain, pills prescribed for extreme suffering.

After all these explanations, the truth that, as the artist of compromise, I didn't want to face was that what Tram wanted was nothing peculiar to her condition, but rather what most of us long for, in quiet desperation behind blinds. But we do not dare to name our desire, in case the power to grasp it eludes us. In laying her own desire naked, my cousin laid bare the root of all our human failings.

After we passed our teenage years my quiet cousin spoke less and less, and her attempts at love grew fewer and more resolute. It seemed to me that my cousin assayed the world of men with determination, but without hope.

Tram finished high school with barely three CXC passes to her name, boxed about for a couple of years, drifting from low-paying job to low-paying job with no particular interest, then declared that she wanted to go abroad. My mother, who had assumed primary responsibility for her after my grand-mother was no longer able to manage, arranged with her eldest brother, our Uncle Dunstan, to file for her to go to the USA, where she trained and found work as a phlebotomist. My uncle wanted her to go to college but Tram had no interest in being cooped up for long periods within doors in classrooms in a country where doors opened only to let people in or out.

I thought her being a phlebotomist had a ring of poetic rightness about it. My cousin was a woman who dealt in blood. No skin, no surfaces, and not even bone, which locked you in, only blood, which could flow up as well as down, which lay inside the body like a lake in which one lived or could drown.

During these years we kept in touch, mainly because I telephoned her often, and so I had a pretty good idea (my haunted imagination fed over the telephone by the ghosts of her words) of how she was doing, of how her love life, or lack of it, was going, and of the fact that she hated America.

But finally, she stopped answering my phone messages, and in the spring of 2020 she sent me a card inviting me to her wedding. With characteristic speechlessness, not by telephone, but by snail mail and card, my cousin invited me to her wedding. I was not only deeply hurt but devastated because I had not seen this coming; imagination and the sonic waves had failed me. I had not even known she met a man about whom she was serious. Afterwards, when I allowed myself to face the truth, I admitted that her silence meant that he was real. We are superstitious about everything we think is real. Tram was afraid that if she spoke her prince in words, either some malevolent fate would spirit him away from her or he would crumble into dust when his image hit air.

She didn't send me any photographs, and I never asked.

I wasn't able to go to the wedding because I fell dangerously ill and would have died, but in the end I wasn't able to stand it and in the summer of 2020 I arrived in the US to see my cousin.

Tram came to the airport alone. I hugged her and felt tears on her face.

'Tram why are you crying? Is it from happiness? Yu heart bruk with happiness to see me?' I was laughing as I said this but she nodded against my shirt.

'So Daniel gone to work,' I said casually as we sat in the back of the taxi taking us from Dulles Airport into Frederick, the

Maryland suburb where she and Daniel had a house. It was the first time his name had been mentioned and it sat like a bridge of invitation between us. But, for the first time, I was tongue-tied by my cousin's tongue-tiedness; I didn't want to force her to say things she didn't want to say. (Struck dumb, like any half-witted schoolboy). Her husband taught art at a regular school and today, when I was coming to visit her for the first time in seven years, was a Saturday. Yet she said he went to work.

'Yes,' she said without explanation, and she was smiling at me, her eyes radiant either with happiness to see me or with her happiness as Daniel's wife. She had not kept in touch with Uncle Dunstan, who lived in another state, and the rest of the family was not good in keeping up with her silence. Some, my sisters B and Mitch, thought her ungrateful.

'So I won't get to meet him till later today, or tonight.'

'Tonight,' she said, her glistening eyes still trained on my face. She was even more beautiful than I remembered, her naturally star-apple-coloured mouth (she had never worn make-up) in spectacular relief against her perfect chocolate skin. She still had high, wide cheekbones and vaguely slanted eyes like Nefertiti's. Was still fine-boned and slender but with a secret roundness to her body that said she was a woman satiated on love. She still had the sexiest backside I had ever seen on a woman, and when she walked it hurt because it was the rear-end of a woman you could tell had a man. Being older suited her. She looked quiet and still, not quiet and wild like when we were kids.

'Mama sends her love, and all manner of nyamings. Roast breadfruit, dookunnu, Christmas cake – she keep it for you from last year – sorrel and fry fish. I thought they would arrest me for contraband at US Customs. Really nerve-wracking, but you know I could not disappoint Mama. I just decided if they took the stuff off me I would stand there and eat as much of it as I could, so I could tell her, without having to lie, that it was enjoyed.'

Her rare laugh broke out, sudden and sweet. 'I somehow don't think it would have been so much fun having to gobble all of that standing in an airport line.'

I was studying her face and she blushed, looking away. 'So Mama well?' she said.

'Yes, she well, and cantankerous same way. Still saving Miss Wilhell and Miss Celestina from demself an dem husband. She seh to tell yu she sorry you couldn't get the country chocolate, but di wukliss boy (that's me) refuse to carry it. That was the one thing I decide I not tekking, even for Mama. Mi sure they would think mi have weed hide in deh. So, sorry, mi chile, no *chaalklit* tea fi yu tidday.'

Her laughter was very happy and I knew she wanted me to talk about the family, to bring them to America for her, so I talked all the way, bringing B, Peaches and Munchie; the redoubtable Evangeline; Mitch (for the one Micheline); Truck, Vicki and Davidow; Uncle Desmond and Fedora, Lemuel and Jackson; Kadian, Lamont and Fergus and their parents Aunt Rita and Reedy; Kyla, Joseph, Marcia and Benjamin with Uncle Titty and Aunt Mouse; Winston, Katie and Morat; Carol, Jason, One Son, Violet, Brown Gal and their various offspring to her, peeling them out of their wrappings the way we would later peel the dookunu and fry fish, watching her face so hungry for them, that involuntarily my mind went back to the days in her room in our far district, Cedar Valley, in Jacaranda backabush when, with the burden of love and prophecy, she underwent enormous transformations. Had this man been enough for her, or not, or had we become one of the faraway places that now she needed, the way a haemophiliac needs blood? But for a moment, a few hours, the world was a round glass in which we two were held, a globe made by the intoxicating bubble of our words of reunion, or rather my words of it and her laughter, her silence and cries, the provender from home holding us anchored and deep, so the world we made that day did not float away but was chained at its bottom to the sea I had flown across, the same sea that cradled our islands. In the house I felt the shadow of Daniel's presence but we did not speak of him as we moved through the dim and shadowy rooms until he came back that night. There was, for a magical moment lifted out of time, only us, and home.

If anything reminded me that the propensity of time was

like the propensity of seawater to reclaim the dump-up where they build house and call it city, it was the collection of old-fashioned clocks on the shelves in the little nook she called her den.

'You're quite a collector,' I said, astonished, studying up close the hourglass with the half-fallen mercury. 'When?'

'Just after I met Daniel,' she said. 'Come and have some lunch. Mek wi eat Mama fry fish.'

'Hi,' Daniel said. 'Glad to see you.'

I looked at Tram. Smiling, she murmured something about heating up his dinner and went into the kitchen. Leaving us alone, or me alone, with this shock.

No photographs. Ever. And she hadn't told me Daniel was a boy from home.

Things I hadn't remembered since forever. Hadn't wanted to remember. The Pritchards lived at the edge of the district, place we called Canepiece. Not because it had any cane growing but because it was real backabush, nowhere near civilization. In a district where most of us were poor and struggling, the Pritchards were ultra poor. And not just poor. Tief. I could hear Mama's voice as she lifted up her hand to heaven and dropped it to make the sign of the cross. 'The tiefingest set of hootiah ever God allow to walk this earth. Tief milk outa coffee.' They were reputed to be inbred, because nobody else wanted to join themselves to a family so badbreed. Diseases we knew nothing about in the 1990s were reputedly rife among the Pritchards: tb, palsy, head lice, hookworm, even yaws, which went out with slavery.

We are six years old and Tram is coming into the yard leading a boy by the hand. Maaga-est boy I ever see in my life, so maaga he's bent like a safety pin when I bend it to make a hook fishing for eel and mullet in the river below my grand-parents' house.

Tram takes the boy to Gramps who is sitting on the verandah step chipping out a new mortar to grind coffee beans.

'Him hungry, Grampa,' Tram says.

'Eh?'

'Hungry, Grampa. Feed him.'

The boy looks ashamed but he takes the bread and peanut butter Gramps gives him, stands holding it by his side looking foolish.

'Eat it, son,' Gramps urges him, in his gruff, kindly way.

The boy mutters something incomprehensible.

'Him seh him wi' eat it when him go home, Grampa,' Tram announces confidently, as if she is this boy's mouthpiece. She is still clinging possessively to his skinny arm which is pitted with mosquito bites.

Even then I was jealous. I was jealous again twice, when I saw him pushing the swing in the schoolyard with her in it during recess. We quarrelled. That is to say, I quarrelled, Tram walked away, fierce and speechless for days. I accused her of consorting with nasty nayga, tiefing people. I wooed her for three days with marble, top, otaheiti apple before she came back to me. I always felt she came back only because the boy had disappeared.

I saw him again once, twice, in our teens. A well-off branch of Pritchards had adopted him and taken him to live in the capital, Kingsport. He came to visit his family in the summer at first, and then not again. The family boasted later that he was bright, could draw, won some art scholarship to some school in America. The district laughed. Could anything good come out of Nazareth?

My cousin had yearned after faraway places and come to America – not so far when you think about it – to take up with a canepiece prince. Talk about full circle. God Almighty.

Daniel Pritchard. She had told me her married name was Pritchard, but I would never have guessed. We called him Bugsy. Everyone knew him by his pet name, Bugsy.

Did Uncle Duncan know? And decided to keep quiet?

He wasn't skinny. Short, thick and red, the way all the Pritchards were red. Paunch (I noticed with satisfaction, comparing my own rather spectacular abs), big shoulders, delicate hands and feet like a woman, thick crude mouth, eyes sink-in under hole like slug under rockcliff.

'Oh, so yu a yard-boy.' If he picked up a double entendre, too bad.

The sink-in eyes looked knowing, faintly amused. He picked it up all right. 'Yes. Tramadol didn't tell you?' He gave her her full name. No one else I knew did. It made me unaccountably angry.

'Tramadol didn't tell you?' and I realized I had made a bad mistake. The thought that he knew Tram kept secrets from me, the thought that he might think Tram was ashamed and take it out on her, both were unbearable to me. Yu damn fool, Petey.

'Yeah,' I said, buying time. 'Yeah, yeah. So the man – doing good.'

'Well, not bad, you know? Can't complain.' His work was exhibited in galleries. And it was all over the house, couldn't be missed. Wild, angry canvases of fire and ice, swirls, coils and serpentine ropes of colour that shouted in the shadowy rooms where they kept the blinds closed to keep out the heat of the real, not the pictured sun; clashing tornadoes; the screaming blue hearts of hurricanes; among green fields, vast wastes of red and golden desert so fierce the eyes, the soles of the feet, burnt; lava streams and seas that seemed to explode with gunpowder; lakes of white ice under coconut palms – and all of this outpouring of impossibilities imagined was layered over the face of a woman that was always there in the background, Tramadol's face pocked with stalks and tendrils from the ends of which these crashing, pulsating motions erupted – they were swirling in and out of it, towards and away from it, within and without of it, breaking apart its contours and the canvasses' borders.

He had made her into an idol, the cliché called Muse, or his slave. God Almighty, did she spend all her days sitting for his productions?

'Can't complain.'

'Tramadol tells me you went into computer programming.'

'Yes. Run a small business in Kingsport.'

'Your own?'

'Yep.'

'Good, man,' he said, super-hearty. I raised my eyebrow

35

and he looked embarrassed. 'I mean, that's really good. Things can be so hard, you know, back home; it's good when a man don't have to work for anybody.'

'Back home not so back, you know. Anybody can make it if they really want to,' I lied. Who di bc this – Pritchard boy – think he is?

Tram came back in with the dinner, my mother's things from home. Her eyes were bright, very bright, on my face.

Be patient for the story of this love. It gets kind of bloody.

I was there for one week. It should have been two but I cried obligation and fled to Uncle Dunstan's in Florida.

I wanted to believe she waited on him hand and foot, but she did not. She went to work three days a week and when she came in, late, because three days meant she had to cram forty hours into three fifths the normal space, he prepared their dinner and washed the plates as well. He used one of the second-floor bedrooms as his studio. For sunlight. If he worked in the morning she brought him his lunch; tiptoed in the house and he could not be disturbed. King of the Kong. Thank God my room was in the basement so I didn't have to tiptoe around no king.

I wanted to believe that sitting for him daily she had no life, but she didn't sit for him. Like a peasant with a bucket and a well, he had drawn up all her secrets out of her deep depths where they had been hidden, and splashed them out on his one acre. There they were, down pat on his palette, spread out like bundles the homeless foraging on the street have picked through and left open. No need to gaze again at her face to remember them. No, she didn't sit for him.

On the days she did not go to work she gardened and minded her clocks, while we talked (ridiculously, in hushed tones if it was in the house), or she showed me around Maryland and Washington, going out in the car I rented (I could not bring myself to drive his, and she didn't own one; she didn't want to drive). She was not as silent as she had been, but she said less. We talked and were companionable together, just like old times, and I knew she wasn't there. In the middle of sentences she broke off, went almost into those trances I

36

remembered, but she wasn't looking into the heart of revelations. She was thinking of Daniel. We'd be sitting in a café in downtown DC sipping juice and waiting for dessert, and all of a sudden, she gone. She never got up right away; she would wait several moments, even half an hour, and then she would say, regretfully, or hurriedly, with a sudden agitation, like someone who has been delivered a message from far: 'Pete, I have to get back.' But I knew from the first broken sentence that she wanted to go back to him. He called her as securely as if he had a cord tied under her rib; she came skittering back; she would run at top speed through the labyrinthine maze to the mouth of the cave where he waited.

I didn't see many books. She said she hardly read any more, because it was so hard to find new books that had unforgettable characters. Modern books had only unforgettable words, or attempts at words. She said if she read at all now, it was the books she read as a child – always, she said, only rereading.

'Tram, yu come a Merica come regress?' I said it like a question, a joke, but she knew I was serious.

'I prefer the garden,' she said.

She had never shown any interest in the gardens our grandmother and my mother planted, but now she was obsessive about pushing her bare hands into the soil, making sure it was warm and wet, about cradling the new seedlings in little pots of earth under plastic canopies. She planted flowers, bright seasonals and hardy perennials spreading from the vast yard to right up against the house, a lake of blooms, burning fire and ice, that climbed avidly over the porch railings and seethed at the front door, as if they were under enormous pressure to break it down and mingle with the cataclysmic landscapes flowing out of their frames into the hallway from the studio upstairs.

She had a part, a corner off by itself like a shrine, where there were only flowers that grew in Jacaranda: Joseph coat, croton, hibiscus, trumpet lily, broomweed and some things that at home didn't have a name and grew wild in bushes but were sold for expensive prices in America. She circled that part off with stones.

At the exact centre, as if she had measured it, a sundial. Or an imitation of one. Twenty-first century. Made in USA.

The smell in the summer was sickly sweet. Butterflies zig-zagged, drunk; bees hit the ground heavily, without sound.

Among the flowers she sowed tomato, cucumber and herbs. Thyme, skellion, marjoram, rosemary (Pray you, love, remember).

'Daniel has a nervous stomach. The best way to do organic is to do it yourself.'

I thought she wanted children, and the garden was a compensation. 'We are not ready for children, not yet. Not for another ten years, at least.' Not for another ten years, at least. A woman's biological clock ticks in one direction only, no rewinding, and the man telling her they will not be ready for children in ten years? Either the bredda had mumps as a child or he was a selfish bastard.

The garden took up a great deal of her time. But the clocks were his only rival. Every night, rain or shine, he left her there in the den polishing clocks. She dusted them all, one by one, with a soft chamois, before she went to their room.

Thirty-seven clocks, each from a different era; and, in all, fourteen countries. She was aiming for fifty two, one for every week in the year. Some she had collected for herself; others friends had brought back from their travels in other places.

'Friends? You've changed a lot, Tram.'

'Not really. No, maybe. People I know, co-workers, friends of mine and Daniel's, people from church, when they going anywhere I ask them to look out for me, if they see a clock that look old.'

'People from church? Nuh tell mi seh yu go church now.'

'Yeah, mi go. Mi start go from about three year now.'

Clock and church. The three years of her marriage.

'Mi jus think yu mus turn thanks. Granma Pointy used to seh. Life short. Mi go fi turn thanks.'

She went because she was happy. People go to church when they can't manage. She went because she was happy.

'So tell mi bout di clock dem now.'

'This one I got from Toronto. We went there for one of

Daniel's exhibitions. Actually one of the artists made it; it was part of his exhibit. Cost a mint, but it was worth every penny.' I'm looking at her hands delicately handling the construction of chrome and wood. I think of her holding an infant. 'This one, you wouldn't believe. Yard sale down the road from us, the people were throwing out a whole roomful of old time stuff because they wanted to modernise, and right there underneath a pile of Amish slipcovers that I was digging up out of curiosity, not intending to buy anything, just digging up, this incredible replica of an ancient Egyptian water clock that they said someone had brought them years ago from Egypt.'

It wasn't what I had meant.

The Egyptian water bowl was beautiful, ochre clay scrolled with hieroglyphs in beaten bronze that I recognized from the Book of the Dead, which she was reading from the age of ten.

The sundial and the hourglass were gifts from Daniel. Given on two birthdays.

'So what, yu feel him go lef yu one day, and all o dis – dis clock ting – is countdown?'

I didn't need her serious acceptance of the question to feel like a dog. Shame followed the words out of my mouth.

'Life short,' she said, soberly. 'When yu happy, yu want to remind yourself not to get too – what yu used to call it again? Hubris.' She was smiling, laughing at herself, her ungrammatical use of the word. 'Too hubris.'

'I'm sorry, Tram. I shouldn't have said that. It was unfor-givable.'

'Hush.' She stood on tiptoe, put her finger on my mouth. Trailed fire where she didn't touch. 'Come. Mek wi go get some lunch.' And as she moved off towards the kitchen (my manship in one hell of a preckeh) it struck me how often she used food as a bridge and how often it was a way of showing that she pitied me. And I was torn between the contemplation of that and the fact that my cousin in the grip of happiness chose to keep the skull of time grinning in myriad poses from her mantelpiece.

Wait on the story of this love. It will eventually cut away flesh; it grows to the bone.

The transformations I witnessed that summer were of a different kind.

She was both transparent and fleshed. Among her flowers her skin became preternaturally sensitive, so that at the end of the day you could see their impress, like tattoos, on her face, her neck, the exposed parts of her arms. They faded only slowly, always leaving a pale hint of themselves behind, so that her edges appeared ghostly. One evening I was afraid as the sun fell. She was standing beside the sundial and as its shadow fell across her I saw the pure architecture of her skeleton beneath her clothes. I don't know if it was a vision; I didn't think it was a dream; I knew the image of death was easy for my envious mind to conjure in the face of her obsession with him. I thought of Evangeline and felt a sudden longing for her dark interpretations.

When she was with him, whenever he was nearby or in the same room, her flesh came like glue, viscid and loose, as if unstuck from her bones. Yet she flowed towards him, as if her soul gathered and pooled itself to a centre that was inside him, tight and secret. I used to think that D.H. Lawrence fellow was a perv, writing all those ridiculous things about how women love, but now I wasn't so sure. Maybe there were women like my cousin.

I looked away from her bruised mouth in the morning.

But it was her pity I couldn't bear. She paid homage to our friendship, the way one might honour a beloved relative who has passed on. The friendship we had shared she had given over to him. It was there in the gestures that went beyond sex: the way they spoke without words, the way their hands fell easily into each other's sitting side by side, the way they anticipated each other's thoughts and finished each other's sentences, so that I felt like an awkward guest who had stumbled upon an intimacy in a secret room. The way she had obviously entrusted her most trivial thoughts to him. Oh, she tried, but the truth could not hide: she made room for me in the house of his occupation, as she had made room for me in the basement. I was a welcome and most honoured guest, her eyes brightened with sadness and nostalgia, a sweet and most hurtful longing; I probably fancied a mute plea for – forgiveness? understanding? No doubt a mere fancy, because in all the time I had known her, my cousin never doubted the rightness of her destiny, which she had either chosen or it had chosen her. She was love's votary, without backsliding. If it meant the laying to rest of a friendship (for her pity was for this, not my love, which she never acknowledged), Tramadol was not the one to apologise, or regret.

I came to see that my cousin had chosen not a man who loved her, but a man she loved. Understand me. This is not a statement about whether or how he loved her. It is a statement about why she chose him. (Truth is, I don't really give a damn about him.) To me, this was the worst compromise. Eve's curse, my trenchant sister B would have said ('and thy desire shall be to thy husband, and he shall rule over thee', was B's feminist mantra of warning and favourite Scripture verse). To Tram, it was simply the one hundred percent she had always believed in, going all the way across the burning desert to the lake at the end of the world, no waiting on the bridge halfway for her lover. I saw that she found how much or how he loved her irrelevant. Her fulfilment was in her own feelings.

To be fair to the bredda, he wasn't a bad fellow. Tried his best to be friendly. It was I who wasn't playing ball.

Between us this curious dance of affiliations. Creepy. Nauseating really.

One morning, after a dream of serpents coiled at the foot of a tree in a monstrous garden, I vomited, made my excuses, and left for Florida and the sanity of Uncle Dunstan's home in the Everglades.

From the safety of my uncle's front porch, I write this note in my journal: Here is the story of this love, when all is said and done. There, among her two things (her gardens and her clocks), her impossible love and canvases of lava and ice, my cousin is living more intensely and perhaps more fully than anyone I know.

In the morning the Everglades are burning again, as they do every summer.

★

My cousin had exactly seven years. What, in our superstitious family, is known as a Sabbath of years. At the end of seven years a gyre is complete, something new begins. Christ or Legba crosses at the crossroads, whichever you believe. With instructions. Either a straight line of truth or many conundrums. I often long for the line, but I seem to have lived all my life buffeting the riddles. The member of our family who seems to have got the two together in a comfortable alliance is Evangeline the seer (who does not believe in Legba). 'Hear me, people! The straight line of truth is found in parables. That seeing they may not see, and hearing they may not understand.' Evangeline preaching at Crossroad, the district piazza pale under the one street lamp, the murmuring crowd of her listeners stained with shadow from the colours of Ethiopia, red, green and gold, cast by her Pope's mitre and warner-stick. The rest of us flounder quite a bit.

My cousin had seven years. After Daniel died, she tried volunteerism, then flirted with the convent. Almost took Franciscan orders, according to B's version. Can't be sure, don't know how reliable Dunstan's facts really are. Old man has got Alzheimer's.

★

Today wasn't so good. Had to go out, doctor's appointment. Normally she just stays inside. Basement, because it's coolest. Try not to open the windows. She feels cursed. They said certain things would help. Black cohosh. The tablets bruised her throat, made no difference. She tried the tea, black cohosh in liquid, pooling thick in the cup, like medicine that works. Then soy supplements. No difference. The doctor's office is fiercely air-conditioned; patients, complaining, get goose bumps. The fall is coming; outside, the temperature has dropped. She sweats in the cool interior, as a refrigerator sweats in winter. But the beads of water rolling off her face, her neck, arms, between her thighs, are heat beads, salt and scalding when they fall in her eyes. Other patients look sympathetic, or politely away, or gaze frankly, thinking she may be more sick than they are.

In Jacaranda, old women would have offered her tepid

water, or a handkerchief moistened with Limacol, 'Wipe yuself wid dis, mi dear, nuh mind.'

What she cannot bear, most of all, is the stares. She no longer knows, even when she isn't sweating, whether it is her spectacular looks that draw eyes, or other telltale signs. She wants to glance frequently behind herself, to see if she has messed her clothes, but is afraid to be gazed at, again. (If her clothes are messed, she will be gazed at, regardless. But somehow, being seen glancing behind herself, is too much to bear). On journeys she stops frequently, looking for restrooms where she can inspect herself in safety, away from eyes.

'I think the best thing is the hysterectomy,' the doctor says, busy, glancing at her watch to check the time set down for the next patient. (The waiting room is full). 'No point bleeding to infinity, and you're already severely anaemic. I'll give you a referral.'

She thinks with a shudder of men poking around in her nether parts, seeing only maimed tubing and conduits.

'Can you make it a female doctor, please?'

'Of course.'

Though it may be six of one and half a dozen of the other. She's already quarrelled with the doctor's assistant. She recalls the girl's look of astonished confusion when she pushed the speculum away. 'Where are you going with that, my dear? You planning to examine cow? Find something smaller.'

'But –'

'Just because I am up in age does not mean I have a well underneath there. It is eighteen years since my husband died. Root and cartilage, that is what you will find down there. That thing cannot pass through. Find something smaller. I don't want you to damage me.'

In the end the pap smear is not done because the girl cannot find a smaller instrument. She thinks of being touched, even the lightest of butterfly touches, down there, and shudders. The sight and feel of her own blood terrify her.

She comes back out to pay her co-pay at the counter and she's sure everyone in the still full waiting room has a too-polite look, the doctor spoke too loud and they all heard her business, or her pants are messed again, even though she just checked herself in the restroom.

This paranoia, this terror and conviction of eyes, of being fully exposed, as if crowds are seeing her skeleton under her clothes, is constant and unbearable. She jumps at every touch, someone's skirt brushing hers, passing by; sound as delicate as a leaf falling makes her break out in new sweats. She hurries home to the cool of her basement because only there, in that sanctuary, can she practise slowing her heartbeat and making sure to think no thoughts with feelings. She does not think of the garden unwatered for three days because the pollen makes her hot even in the teal-blue evenings of fall. She veers her mind away from questioning and questioning again whether she has remembered to turn off the stove or lock the front door behind her. She trains herself not to take a taxi so she can get home faster to see. She waits for the bus. Blanking her mind helps her to keep the panic attacks at bay. She is familiar enough now with the changes in her body to know that she alternates heat and cold every twenty-three minutes, if she keeps her mind very very still and empty, but the flashes double in force and frequency if she thinks about these things, or others like them – omissions, mistakes, decisions that may have been wrong or right, the fear of conversation (the telephone ringing unexpectedly, the postwoman knocking to say there's a parcel too big to push through the slot), eyes. The flashes are as clockwork, as her periods used to be. Dead on time.

Her body, which she has scarcely attended (beyond washing, clothing, feeding and occasionally perfuming it) since Daniel went, is now always open to her own eyes – she stretches full length on the daybed, stripped to the skin under the ceiling fan. She keeps the duvet rolled to the foot of the bed so that at a moment's notice (or, to be exact, each twenty-three minutes' notice), she can pull it up over herself, then pull it down again. On, off, on, off, playing musical duvets. Accommodating her actions to the rhythms of heat and cold, fire and ice. She cannot bear the air conditioning, it makes her feel imprisoned when the windows are closed of necessity and not of choice. So she has kept it off, even in sweltering summer.

It is in the nights that she knows her body is no longer hers alone. Inside her skin is another woman, other women, some clamouring for ice; others, desert bred, with burning feet. In the morning they have left traces, huge welts, on her skin.

Twice in the night she gets up to change her incontinence diapers. Regular menstrual pads haven't been enough. They mess the bed. The floor, chair, whatever she sits on. She thinks of the woman with the issue of blood. So desperate she touches the hem of a man's robe, in search of healing. She thinks of the panting, fainting women in Jane Austen and Georgette Heyer. Not whalebone stays. Blood. Blood red and violent, not blue. Blood protesting its raw and vivid self-knowledge, refusing its encagement in common decencies, bandages, napkins, tubes.

She doesn't know which is worst. The mechanical attendance to blood, keeping it in its cage, or the faces in the mirror, or the temptation to blame everything wrong in her personality on this transformation – to do nothing, give in to memory loss, which has been happening ever since she can remember, long before this change; give in to the desire, acknowledged in childhood, to be responsible for nothing – because finally and at last here is a valid excuse. She thinks that men have been using this against women for millennia (Adam in the garden hiding, hiding from the Lord), but the temptation does not go away. She wonders what men feel, in their similar years. Wishes that Daniel were here to tell her. Shudders to think that she might have had to live through that (his), and this (hers), with him. Thank God he is gone. Thank God she is alone. She longs for cool sheets, and sleep. She could not bear now to hug anyone, with the bad smells under her arms and her tits. (Sometimes she misses Pete, quite viscerally, almost wishes she had not sent him away. But not to have done, would have been selfish. And, anyhow, now, she could not have borne even his company).

Her mind takes her back, unwilling, to an image of Aunt Mouse, Seraphine's elder by eight years, lying on her bed, perspiring, saying to her daughter Kyla, 'Read the Bible to me. I'm going. Mi time come.' Aunt Mouse checking her funeral chest to make sure the burial clothes she has laid aside have not been eaten by moth or cockroach; giving irate Uncle Titty instructions about how to dispose her body in the box. After arising from her bed, Aunt Mouse never cooked again. In all the years after, Kyla or Uncle Titty doing the cooking because Aunt Mouse could not stand the stove heat. So this is what happened to Aunt Mouse, she thinks, wondering.

It is said it runs in families. (She wonders why nobody has prepared her for this. Nothing she has heard or read). She asks B. B is surprised to hear from her. I hardly knew anything was happening, B says. Same with Micheline, except that she felt a little more tired than usual. No one they knew suffered unduly. Aunt Titty, reluctantly, had taken hormone replacement. Was all. 'You always have to do things the hard way, ehn, Tram? And you are earlier, much much earlier, than most,' B said, shaking her head over the phone. 'Talk to Mumsy nuh. Hold on, let me give her the phone.'

Her cousins' mother was matter-of-fact, speaking in the low, barely audible voice she remembered. 'Yes, yes, that is exactly how it go. Same as you describe it. It kill some people, yu know.'

It was a relief to hear herself laughing. 'I don't think it get as bad as that, Mama. I never hear of that happening.'

'Hmn, hmn. It happen.'

She thinks of the women of Mama's generation, and all the women in their family before that, and before that, and before. She thinks of the faces in the mirror, the limbs under her skin. Lamias, ol higues, soucouyant. In the old days. Canepiece, rockstone, washtub, old iron, uphill climb with water pan on their heads under the broiling sun. Children in the belly and a long thin line of others walking behind, and the following year another when the one in the belly dropped. They breastfed as long as they could because God's milk was all they could afford and, by nature's serendipity, which they probably did not know, it kept the next child coming, at bay for a while. Hungry, and sometimes the man beating them. Tough as old iron, their hands weathered, their bodies gnarled and sinewy as tree roots from labour under the rain and sun, beating clothes, tying cane, hoeing grung, cooking food, carrying water, bending low to noint baby belly with burn kerosene oil from the tilly lamp to heal or keep away gripe; surely at the end, which came early and fast, the fountain of their blood abruptly dried or rushed out of doors gasping, carrying in its stream the turbid history of their rage. She thought of the exigency of her own life and the passion with which she reached for what they had never had, these women whose lives and deaths Aunt Seraphine, Mama, had told her children in stories. Aunt Seraphine, every misty morning, saying she saw them, long lines of women in slave clothes carrying washpan on their heads following the river's course, singing low. Tramadol has fought with all her might for another vision, another life, but now she comes face to face with the skull at the root of the family's cotton tree.

Other women, generations, millennia of them, their faces leering under her skin in the mirror, their writhing limbs stretching her flesh so that in the morning her stomach is bloated (the doctor says gas) and the skin of her belly and breasts has slipped a little further on its way down south, to the body and burial of bone.

She tells herself there is a pattern, and sets herself to find it. Women's courses are set by the tides, and the moon. And each other. It is a well-known fact that young women living to-gether synchronize their periods. Our family has been too close, she tells herself. It is Evangeline who carries the burden of the spirit, generations of them, from slavery days until now, and look, I carrying the burden of blood. She thinks of Pete, whom she sometimes misses, in the moments when she can bear the thought of company, and she wonders what burden he has been given to carry.

Her body has acquired its own life, and demands a great deal of attention.

She tries for another pattern.

The body is 75% water.

We are seventy-five percent water.

Seventy-five percent body.

She feels that now, stretching out in front of her, is a waste of years, in which seventy-five percent of her thoughts will be on her body, how to fix it, protect it, feed it differently, disguise its inexorable pilgrimage down south, keep it under, not be aware of it, not feel it, its aches, bowel disorders, wayward appetites, rejections of things it had loved, its blood flowing in the wrong directions, too fast and then not at all, skull, bone.

The body is too much with us, late and soon, she says to herself, grimacing.

In the end she thinks there may be no pattern at all, except the signs of the body preparing itself for death. And it is left to her cousin to think, not long from now, that the long reaching after the reconciliation of fire and ice, the fierce relentless agony with which she had reached after love, has also been the sign of the body's struggle with death. Its pilgrimage of preparation. Her life has described a circle.

She no longer goes into the den. She has covered all the clocks with a sheet and allowed them to wind themselves down, so that the house is filled with silence. She moves the mercury-clock, the hourglass, into the basement room with her. The cool, slick silver of mercury falling, with its promise but no delivery of sound, soothes and comforts her.

The signs of the body preparing itself for death. She had not thought before of her body as a place of intelligence, with its own will separate and apart from the one in her mind. She had read that it did, in her Bible, and in the Book of the Dead, but she hadn't really known what they were talking about. She had sought Daniel with every bone and fibre of her being, had consciously and instinctively yielded herself to him, when she found him, but she had not understood her body, that it had made any of these choices for her, until it betrayed her. She finds she likes the thought of this pattern, of an intelligent body preparing itself the way Aunt Seraphine, and Granma and Gramps before her, prepared their burial chests, laying out the right clothes (dignified clothes befitting their age and station), the instructions on exercise book paper (including who and who is not to come to the funeral), the last will and testament (including who and who has been

48

disinherited because of improper behaviour, who they must be buried beside, and who not to bury in the family plot because they are not Pointy or Morris born and bred). Above all, the money for the coffin, to prohibit the disgrace of a mean ceremony.

With this feeling of a pattern she finds that there are compensations. She submits herself, trancelike, to a sense of life finely balanced between yin and yang, parable and revelation, ice and fire.

Food was difficult, and fascinating. She learnt the properties of food and their affiliations in minute ways; which combinations made her flatulent and which made her go; that animal protein was heat producing and cheese and milk taboo; that her upper arms grew fat despite vegetable dinners before six, and exercise; that the secret of eating without bloating her stomach was savouring – that is, chewing small mouthfuls, very fine and slow. She came to appreciate the intimate intricacies of food and its secret lives, stashed and hidden away only for those who are patient to discover. She learnt, with a sense of slow satisfaction, like a connoisseur tasting wine, the pleasure of standing still on a long escalator instead of running quickly up its spine; and because she could no longer walk briskly without getting hot, she found that on slow walks by the creek trail she could see with her naked eye microscopic insects nestled in the cups of leaves, and if she stood very still, very very still, without moving her feet, she could feel the earth crawl. That when she traced the lines in her hymn book she could sometimes see beside hers the finger of God, tracing 'mene mene' (upharsin) or 'let' (there be light) in runnels of fire that lit up her finger bones under the frail flesh. These intensities of calm alternated with the sharp and vivid clamour of physical misery. In these moments of rest, her own company, after a long time of missing Daniel, became again a joy. She thinks, how fortunate, not to have died young, with youth's tragedy, in a car accident or drinking poison for love.

Late one evening she came upon him sitting in the garden, on the bench behind the acacia bush that hid the front of the garden from its back. She was startled, and a little frightened, because she had not seen him in so long. Right after his death, and for the next forty days, he had been in the habit of stopping by for small chats, and to see how she was doing.

'How yu do?' he says with the calm comfortableness with which they had always greeted each other after a long absence, as if neither had really left, not in any way that mattered, and they were settling back into an old routine.

'Why have you come?' Her question puts a wedge between them; she has never questioned their relationship before.

A look of pain crosses his face. He holds out his hands to her, gentle, diffident, and she reaches hers towards him, repentant.

In the night Tramadol is praying.

★

When they found her she was lying in ice water, on her back, a look of bliss on her face. B and Peaches went with me to collect and sort her woman's things. My mother was insistent that there should be no cremation, no matter the expense of flying her home. Though at the time she and I were not talking to each other, she swallowed her spit enough to give me instructions.

'Pete, every Pointy for three generation, bury in this family plot, yu hear. With every bone intact. We want to see her one more time. Bring her home.'

I took the clock of mercury, and we brought her home.

II

DEATH

It has been raining like this for two days, as if the sky has suffered a great wound, and with it a weight pressing down, an unbearable urge to void its contents. The yard is waterlogged. Black moss grows up the sides of the stone flower pots and the house. Weeds and flowers have flourished rankly in the downpour, so that the yard looks wild, abandoned, as if no one, except the snails, has lived there for a long time. The snails are everywhere, though seemingly invisible except in the brief lull between one downpour and the next. When the torrents ease they uncurl from the tight commas into which they have rolled themselves to the roots of plants, and appear on the ground like a ridged carpet. Thick phalanxes inching up the walls leave shiny trails of slime that are inexorably covered over by new cohorts that leave their own trail, which is again overtaken by new clots of arrivals, each after each, like a vast caravan under a moving tarpaulin of wrinkled black. Up close, they look like segments of an outsize, diseased sweetsop, or an encrustation of sores bunched obscenely on skin, like grapes. The water-drums at the side of the house have long since filled, so that the gutter spouts are overflowing; waterfalls spill down the sides of the drums and race to join the streams carving new traces as they rush down the slope that borders the house. The land slips away; inside the house Beatrice can feel the slick mud slide even though she cannot see the banana trees bow and give in, or the breadfruit trees brace themselves for a last stand. She can only imagine the tangle of electricity poles lying across trees and roads, the way the announcer described on her battery radio when she bothered to turn it on hours ago. The dusk has fallen without nuance, the rain quickly blue-blacking it to night.

At her plain kitchen table, the cedarwood smoothly shaved but never polished, Beatrice listens to the drumming on the roof and is reminded of Mr Biswas' chant against the dead, 'Rama Rama, Sita Rama, Rama Rama Sita Rama, Rama Rama Sita Rama…' she catches herself abruptly, realizing she has been saying the chant aloud, as if she too is afraid and not merely keeping time to the beat of rain music.

She doesn't know how long she has been sitting there, in the dark, remembering. Day before yesterday, Micheline's daughter Patricia brought her soup in a huge pyrex, enough to last her two days if she keeps it in the icebox that serves as a backup to the fridge. Since then she hasn't tried to cook or light a lamp. She is not able to talk with anyone because the cell phone signals are down and the landline cables incapacitated, torn up by their roots in the engulfing floods. Micheline will be worrying about her being alone, will be sending the poor child out in the mess again as soon as the rain eases up, with more soup, and the child will come, fey and unprotesting, slipping between the held-back curtain of rain and the drying world like an elf slipping between here and faerie, now and then.

But Beatrice likes the being alone. In this house that she grew up in, lived as a married woman in, brought up her children in; from its doorways, waved them goodbye when they went off after their own fortunes, as young people should. An old house, full of memories but accepting of its own silences. She finds the sitting in the dark strangely comforting. The sound of the rain in the small room has the effect of a blanket. She is drawn close to herself, her thoughts wound about her like a cocoon, not the cage of terror they so often were when she was young. Rather, familiar companions dropping in for a bite to eat, easy at the table or on the living room floor. She thinks that in this atmosphere, if the rain does not ease up for more days, she could bend her mind to what Micheline has asked her to do, recall memories for the children to keep. She doubts she will ever get to the point of writing them down, as Mitch insists. But you never know, Rome wasn't built in a day, and time longer than rope. This rain season is a beginning. Who knows where it might lead?

And yet it might not lead to good. This rain season is out of season, days of floods at the wrong time of year, sea waves driven nautical miles inland so that more and more people have moved to the hills, terrified and hopeless, for the hill houses bring them closer to the dreadful wound in the ozone layer that is shedding its contents in the brimming sea. And the clash of bitterness, the wars between the rich who have owned the hills for generations, and the squatters who have vowed to take them back, these strongholds of the poor, which in the annals of once upon a time were named Sufferers' Heights. Already the days of terror have increased. This house of refuge, one of the last remaining in this last district, may not last. They say there's an atoll in Papua New Guinea that still has clean air. Papua New Guinea now in danger of riches from the sale of visas to Chinese and Americans fleeing to safety. The American government is still trying to stop the trade with threats (up to five years ago Americans needed no visa to Papua New Guinea, where they used to have a military base). But the refugees are not waiting for superpower effects to kick in – desperate, they are buying the visas and migrating in droves. The atoll is crowded, but with some rain forest left. Few Jacarandans could afford a ticket to that different rain.

Rain. Sea. Too much water. Eye water. Last year they buried their mother, Seraphine. John, their father, went before, drawing his knees up in his bed at a ripe old age, as a patriarch should, even one whose mind had gone and left him long ago. A man who had seen into the world nine children, thirty-four grandchildren, ten great grands and counting. Strange how, when the wealthy die, they are remembered by monuments, the mark they have made on the bustling world: Sir So and So, of the Twenty-one Families, passed away on ten, eleven, twenty-nine. Sir So and So was the CEO of Hotel Grandisimo, the Footprints Hotel Chain, Machado and Company, Fuud's Industries. On the radio, when John, a poor man, passes, the roll call of his mark is sounded in plangent flesh, and what is flesh but receptacles of dreams, uncertain potential – the absolute terror of human not-knowing? 'Leaving daughters Evangeline, Beatrice, Micheline, Cynthia (Peaches), Victoria (Vicki), sons Thomas (Truck) and Davidow, sister Beatriss (Mouse), brother Desmond, brothers-in-law Dunstan and Lemuel; thirty-four grandchildren, ten great grandchildren, and many nieces and nephews. Interment in the family plot.' (Though, if we are to be strict about the truth, John was not really a poor man when he passed – not rich, but not poor either, but he had come from poor stock, and lived in humble circumstances. Your children did well, Papsi, Beatrice detours in her mind to tell him). But Pete's name had been missing.

The same roll call marked Seraphine's passing, except that more great grands had been added, and it hurt in a new way that Pete's name had been missing. Seraphine was as rich in death, or as poor, as any man she knew, though in life she had too often acted as though men were above the rest of human-kind, and gave more to her sons than to her daughters, who, Beatrice felt, treated her far better.

And because of this thing with her sons, Seraphine's going, though she had found peace at the end, had been bitter with the taste in her mouth of Pete's name missing.

No parent should have to bury her child, Seraphine said, a recurring sentence in her long quarrel with God. No parent should have to bury her child.

Beatrice rocks herself on the kitchen chair, closing her eyes, feeling the memory of herself rocking Seraphine, thirteen years ago, 'Nuh mind, Mumsy, nuh mind, it awright, it awright, he went in a good way. Don't Avette tell yu how it go? Yu know he went in a good way, in spite of everything.'

And Seraphine, reduced to the devastating helplessness of a child, keening in her daughter's arms, on the verandah step where the snails came up after rain, 'All her life that girl give trouble, cause pain. Is Tramadol, yu know, is Tramadol. I know he going to America because of some foolishness she inveigle him into. I just hope is not scam him getting himself into; yu know how America full of respectable in front and tief an murderation behind.' Beatrice remembers how she held her while she swallow her blood pressure tablet and set her face like a flint, stern and strong, and suddenly she grab herself in her belly as if she could feel the knife blade even then, all those years ahead of time, and she begin to bawl 'Mi son, mi son, mi son, woie, mi son!'

Mumsy don't mind, don't mind, Mumsy, she'd said, he will come back. After all, Merica is not far, just a plane ride round the corner, and she hold her mother and rock her, cursing her brother inside. And was in that moment, seeing her mother cry, her mother who in all the years she know her till then never cry, only set her face like flint in the buffeting of hard times, was then a hard knot form against her brother in her heart and she determine she would never forgive him for what he do to her mother.

She comfort her mother into the night, giving laugh and serving pea soup. When everyone in bed or gone home for the night, she go outside and sit down alone on her mother front step where the snails come up after the rain, and she cry. All our histories our people have been running away to foreign when trouble come, like the only fight we can fight is guerilla war, run away so we can live to fight another day. So we tell wiself. And she crying for larger than her mother's losses or her brother running away, she cry because she wonder if black people doomed to travel all the days of their lives, always have to sit down and weep by Babylon river, simply because their foreparents were forced to cross big water at the point of guns. And the joke is, you don't even see the point of all that running away. Keep running only to return to the point of wi entanglement. She think bout how Tram she run 'way to America, only to marry that half-starven Pritchard boy from Mocho-bottom, and years later she live to think bout how Pete come right back home, come get himself mix up wid a Bypass woman, bitter as gall, that wreck him to hell and back again. She say to sheself what the point, nuh might as well him did stay in foreign an have affair with Tram?

She rises from the table in sudden agitation, moves across to the china buffet to find matches and the Home Sweet Home lamp she inherited from Seraphine a year ago, which Seraphine had inherited from her mother Icilyn, and Icilyn from her own mother before her. Her movements are slow; she is a big, heavy-fleshed woman well up in the middle years, and moreover, at this moment, her bones feel weighted with the remembrance of salt. She watches the faint tremble in her hands as she strikes the match, watches the spark take on the wick and the tongue of flame lick itself from small and wavering to full and steady, gold with the dark penumbra in the centre. She puts the lampshade back on with excessive care, waiting for her hands to quiet. She had thought to bring to memory Seraphine's more serene years, so long after Pete's death, her burial and ceremonial tombing, but instead her mind has slipped around a corner away from the leash her will had put on it, and dug up the memories that it wanted, not the ones it was told. And look what it brought up: half a glimpse of Mumsy mourning immediately after Pete's death, then veering, skittering away, without rhyme, without reason, to the day on the steps when Mumsy received Pete's telephone call, and then all over the place to things she used to think in the future that came after that. You was always a stubborn, unmanageable bugger, Beatrice admonishes her mind wryly. But she is disturbed. She realizes what it means: that she is far from ready to face this memory that is to be faced, twenty years on.

If truth be told, Beatrice Morris, you are lying all the way. Yu just lie, lie. Is not even Seraphine's death you can't face, is Pete's. That's where you meant to begin, where you *have* to begin, and where you can't go.

So you begin at the day when Mumsy get the call from Pete.

Let me go along where it leads, she thinks. Let me call this the beginning. Mitch will just have to put it together how she want; she is the one who want this story, not me, and anyway is she is the one who has made a living out of telling lies, so no problem for her to fix it how she want.

Slowly she returns to the kitchen table, puts the lamp down in the exact centre, because B is a neat freak, goes to the window and peers out at the curtain of rain and the inky, downbeaten trees. A flash of lightning zigs across the yard, its shape and path vividly visible. In the moment of its passing she sees blobs of fallen fruit snagged ghostly in the trashed foliage on the ground: round mangoes glowing like moons; here and there a premature breadfruit, and plums littering the grass. She drops the gauze curtain and goes back to the table to await the clap of thunder. It comes before she is seated again, a mighty clatter like cannon volleys, or the earth's belly shaking. Beatrice shivers and concentrates determinedly on her memories.

I say, let me begin at the beginning. In the summer of 2020, Pete went to visit his cousin, our cousin, Tramadol, really, in a manner of speaking, our sister, in her marital home in Maryland, USA. None of the family knew what transpired except that Pete returned home two weeks later, morose and silent, so much so that Peaches joked, 'Look like Tram obeah yu again, ehn, Pete? Yu even silenter than she now.' You can always depend on Peaches for a bad joke.

Pete gave her a look and walked off without a word. His way. The next day he returned to Kingsport and six weeks later a telephone call came through for Mumsy, Pete on the line, telling her he had sold up his computer business and was going to America. Not just going for a visit. Relocating. Mama start to pant and Truck had to run for a chair and her blood pressure medicine. She was already hurting from Tram's behaviour, how the girl go away for all those years and nary a line to say dog, how yu do; if it wasn't for Pete keeping in touch over everybody's dead body, we would not even have known she was married. And poor Mumsy had lost Evangeline, too, in a manner of speaking, for though Vangie visited often and treated her like new china, I think my mother never forgave herself for giving Vangie away, and she always had this thing that there was some kind of wall between her and her eldest daughter, that would never be broken down, so she could cross over. The rest of us never saw it, at least on Vangie's side, but there was my mother for you. (But the truth is, which of us really knew Vangie all that well, much less as well as a mother's intuition could boast it did?).

And now Pete. Her eldest son. Who, though she tried hard to disguise it, was absolutely her favourite and that was that.

Nothing you can do about the heart's choices, when all is said and done.

Pete stayed in America, living with Uncle Dunstan in Florida, for four years. During this time, I have to confess he didn't behave the way Tram did, he kept in touch with the family, always phoned Mumsy and had long conversations with her on her birthday and Mother's Day. And he came home at Christmas, twice. But, in what to me was simply the way of men, he never spoke about himself, or about Tramadol, and Mumsy feared the worst. Sure, he was living in Florida and Tram was in Maryland a whole plane ride away, and as far as we knew she was still married, but what was the meaning of Pete's silence and what were they doing together that could not be spoken? These were questions my mother asked, fretting herself. We were busy living our own lives – getting married, bearing children, some of us going to school and college, and we were too used to the saga of Tram and Pete, Psyche and Trim, Batty and Bench, and as I said, Man and Man Self, to view any of this with the alarm with which my mother viewed it. We didn't think about it, until the diaries. The one thing we couldn't understand was why my brother threw up a perfectly good small business of his own to go and work for white people in America.

In the beginning, he and I had words about his leaving, bitter words.

'Why yu put Mumsy through this, Pete?' I confronted him the first Christmas he came home. 'Tram lef an never send back a word, an now you run after her, yu tail up in the air like when puppy hear dem call him fi eat food, and all yu give her is six weeks notice? Yu think dat good enough?'

He looked at me in speechless fury and was walking away but I stood my ground, blocking the doorway between the living room and the verandah. 'Why yu have to leave, Pete? What over dere for you? Yu don't have a country?' And it hurting mi bad, because is not just because of mi mother, is because of how everybody running away, going to foreign like dem fool-fool.

Him face twist into a unrecognizable mask, an him tell me

a nasty badword an push past me, leaving me standing there stunned. The person I knew never cursed, no matter how much you provoked him (And I knew I could be damn provoking, I have no qualms to say so). So, on top of everything else, my brother had even become a stranger – so soon. My mother's heart had reason to break.

It was Mitch who found the diaries.

Seeing her with him made me realize I could go at any time. Always wanted to see the rest of the world. Not just like a tourist. I mean see, really see it. I thought if I stayed away I would forget her. At any rate, forget in the way that mattered. But what does that Kris Kristofferson song say… Freedom's just another name for nothing left to lose. I found I had nothing left to lose, because I didn't matter to her that much. This sort of thing pares life down to the bone. I could be anywhere, any time. America was as good a place as any. So I left.

......

The mind's a fine and terrible place. Haunted by the thought (most unfair, most untrue) that maybe, subconsciously, America is the only place, because she's there. Which would mean I'm still hoping there's everything left to lose. How many kinds of a jackass can a man turn himself into? You know?

I still feel my face get hot with shame and the terror we felt, or at least I felt, don't know about Mitch, she never gives anything away, when we sit down there in that room and read a man private thoughts that we not suppose to read and him never mean for us to read and if him never dead we couldn't did read. It tek a long time, maybe longer than some of us live, to realize what Evangeline always seh, dat yu bredda is not yu bredda an yu sister is not yu sister but two separate human being dat yu have to hold sacred and from a distance with awe. And if this is how it should be, somebody explain to me then why when smaddy fi yu dead, your own body turn into a dead weight and lie down like a wound? Why yu feel the weight of death in your own limbs so yu cannot breathe or get up, like is you dead or get the death wound?

Evangeline was the only one who wasn't bothered by Pete's leaving. She quarrelling with us in her Jacaranda-British or vice-versa accent. 'How you all get involve in the big man business? Him don't tie to him mother apron string, is he? Part of the problem with this family is that you all live in each other's pockets. Six families and you all live in the same district and your children eat dinner in their grandparents' house. Is foolishness.'

But Evangeline never grow with us, and she find her all-sufficiency in her God. Is a lot of things Evangeline don't understand.

Pete come home again after the four years, driven by a restlessness him could not contain. He set up back his business in Kingsport, and for a while it seem as if things settle down and he ok. Was after Tram's husband death, two years later, we see the change in him from which there was no turning back. He go up to the funeral. Me, Evangeline and Mitch go as well to give Tram family support. Mumsy couldn't go because from Vangie born she fraid of flying. We try to coax Tram to come home with us to get away from things for a while, but she refuse. Pete stay behind after the rest of us, and he come home weeks later with a shadow on him that mek me feel fraid.

The nearest thing I remember to how Pete was that time, was the time after Tram die, after he and Mitch and me go to bring her home.

She can still remember his silence, the scalding hot tears he wept on the mercury clock he took away for himself from the bizarre collection Tram had on the mantelshelf in what B still thinks of as Tram's fetish room. She can still see his head bent against the wall like something inside him was broken forever.

And indeed something was, B murmurs to herself in her kitchen, where the rain muffles sound to rumour.

She felt his tears would sear the room with their salt heat. She remembers being vaguely surprised that she did not see them smoke or hear them hiss like moisture dropped on a hot grill. Mitch was in the living room, out of sight. B remembers how she was frightened because she could not touch the depths of this despair, and because she didn't know what to do, she said, bracing and abrasive, 'Is awright, Pete, is awright,' and when he didn't respond she went up to him and touched him on the shoulder. He shrugged her off and she tried to put her arms around him, silently cursing her big breasts that got in the way, caused men not to take her seriously if she hugged them without lust. She thought her breasts, which all her life embarrassed her, so that she spoke loudly all the time, would send her brother a wrong signal that she was mothering him, rather than offering sisterly comfort. All of that flew out of her head because the face he turned to her was so terrible that she cried out and hurried from the room. She never told Micheline, though Mitch looked at her face and asked, 'Is what happen, B?' She was remembering the time he cursed her.

Even then, she was ashamed that they set Pete's grief apart from their own, treating him as if he was the one in need of comfort and Tram had not also been their sister. In acknowledging Pete's greater loss, they judged themselves guilty of not loving Tram enough, and dared not look, as their mother did, upon the passion he wasn't supposed to feel.

Disturbed by the memory, feeling vaguely angry at her own emotion, B gets up from the table again, paces the room and rummages in the cabinet drawer under the window; when she sits back down she has, without knowing, lit a candle, which burns low beside the Home Sweet Home lamp. It is a short fat white candle in a steel-grey tin canister. It gives off a faint aromatic smell, like clean linen.

To tell you the truth I wasn't going to get myself involved in this preckeh that Mitch insist on, but I change my mind because of the foolishness people spread around the district, foolishness that I don't want my two children and my grandchild to be carrying as the legacy they have from their best uncle. It surprising to me how birth and death is the quickest way to bring out malice in people. Maybe is a psychological gene throw back from slavery, when bringing any child into the world was a terror, and death was sure and early and brutal; maybe we learnt cynicism then. People spread all sort of rumour based on how they see the family, as if we are backward or mad. They have it to say Pete kill himself because he mad over Tramadol, just as how, according to them, Tram dead because she mad over man. They say Pete seek out his own death on purpose, though he don't exactly lift his hand and do it himself. They say Pete go to foreign and get involve in gang – can you imagine, my decent respectable brother – and gang member follow him back to Jacaranda and kill him for two-timing them. Yet plenty people in the neighbourhood where Pete live, and right here too in this district, know is who do it, Avette testify to it, witnesses see when my brother blood run out of the yard and into the street and climb up the hill to the JP house to give warning, long before the police come. Yet they lie. Because in those days everybody was afraid and they feel that if they spread a lie and call it truth they will be safe; nobody will come and threaten their life for giving witness to the truth. And God Almighty know Jacaranda was a terrible and dreadful place for justice in those days, how many man of law tek graft to look the other way so that their eyes don't see?

Is true that after Tram died, Pete was never quite himself again. He blamed himself bitter for her death, and for a long time afterwards he was in therapy, saying over and over to Mitch who took him there, 'I abandon her, I leave her alone, is my fault she died, I kill her', which just goes to show how useless psychotherapy is for divining the truth, because all that came up out of the depths was what everybody already knew, that Pete killing himself with guilt over Tram, and that it made no sense at all because of course he had had nothing to do with her death nor had he, as he put it, abandoned her. Wasn't all of my mother's trouble over them both how unhealthily close they were even after her marriage and how impossible he had seemed to find it to let her go? A great deal of his self-flagellation come from the fact that he never believe the autopsy report that she die of an aneurism while lying in the bath; him convinced she drown herself in frenzy of despair.

Was no use asking, as a reasonable person would, 'But Pete, how could she have drowned herself when they found her face up and no water in her lungs?' because Pete was not a reasonable person but a Pointy on one side, flush with the family madness and obsessive gene. And especially he would believe anything about Tram; if you told him she could fly he would believe it and as far as he was concerned, drowning without benefit of water (in the lungs or otherwise), was a very simple feat for Tram to perform, just because she was pretty. Beauty is a talisman that can open sesame to every song and dance and fairy tale. That is how the man portion of our species fool-fool. I wouldn't even mention the idiot Jackson who I tie myself to and, thank God, divorce, nine years to the month, now.

Pete himself was quite beautiful to behold but it never opened any doors for him, except the doors to heartbreak and a whole heap o' foolish decisions.

The story of how he came to lose his life didn't begin either with Tram's death, it began long before that. You could go back to the time they were like batty and bench together when we were children, or not so far back, to the time she was married, the time I am remembering about, when him pack up bag and pan, foot and footage, and tek off to America, running away from the very thing him was running towards. Or it begin with whatever it was that Tram tell him after her husband death, that set him on the last roller-coaster down to madness. So, true, you could say Tram caused it, or the bond with Tram he had, that never seemed to go away, at least not from him.

But in another way you could say what happened to Pete was the kind of thing that was happening to every family in Jacaranda during that time. I don't know a single person who was not touched in some way by the bloodthirsty murderationing that made our country more famous in those days than it was famous for its athletes or its musical stars. If was not your father, was your brother, or your husband, or your cousin, or your nephew, or your sweetheart, or your mother, or your sister, or your daughter, or your friend sweetheart or your friend relative or your friend friend. Everybody knew somebody who had been killed. That was what Mumsy said, once. 'Never know the killing going on in the country woulda touch mi.'

How Jacaranda get there I don't know, and I don't plan to be speculating on it now. Basically I don't think we was any different from the rest of the world. Is what Evangeline would call the signs of the end-times, was a trend in the world, but we get it big and nuff, or it look bigger and nuffer in our small country which I learn is the third most populous in the Americas, next to Merica and Canada, too much people per square inch, so of course every fly that pitch, pitch pon us all. And because we born spectacular, as Mitch say, never satisfy with our lot in life but always hoeing down the sides of this confining island to push boat out to sea, we have to be first even in rate and style of murdering. The criminal-dem want to be as famous as the athletes and the musicians and the bright people, I swear to God. That is what I really believe. So maybe in a sense is true that, in the wounded world, Jacaranda have the third biggest wound.

It not any easier to think about these things than to think about what happen to Pete. Mercy Jesus, mercy Lord, how wi living, how wi come through?

The rain has slowed to a drizzle. The pit-pat-pit of water dripping into steady pools replaces the thunder and shreeee! of torrents beating the roofs and gutters. Beatrice does not hear. There are two candles of the kitchen table beside the lamp. She doesn't know how or when the second one got lit, or why.

When Pete come back from America after Tram husband funeral, Peaches say is better if him did stay, for all the communication him communicate with the family. Hardly talk to anybody, Mumsy lucky if she hear from him in a month. And he book himself into therapy. That was the first time he do it. The second and last time was after Tram death. And as far as I could see, the therapy fail that time same as how it fail the second time. But after that first therapy fail, he get very close to Evangeline. Whenever he came down our way he make a beeline straight for Evangeline house in Bypass, and is her house him stay till him ready to go up again. But was a man who always like to do the right thing to semi-please everybody, so he always dropped by us, or more especially by Mumsy, on his way back, never staying so long that we would need to prepare a bed for him, and sometimes scarcely a food bag, though the family land was teeming with ground provisions, vegetables and fruit. He was always in a hurry.

Peaches wondering if Evangeline going turn him into jump-up parson. 'That boy was always a damn monk.' She ominous and irate. 'I don't like the look of how him follow-following up Evangeline at all.'

My mother said nary a word. When he turned up on her doorstep she feed him and sit down and laugh at his jokes that he giving without meeting her eyes, and she say the foolish things that mothers say to their sons that get Mitch and Peaches and me rahtid, because she was so damn racist against her daughters and sun shine out of anything name boypickni. Hear her, 'Yu maaga, yu need smaddy fi cook fi yu. Poor yu. Wait fi some curry goat fi carry up wid yu nuh. Nuh lef di dookunnu, yu can put it in the fridge and it serve yu fi di week. Poor you. Yu need smaddy fi cook fi yu.' Of course that was code for why don't you get married, for though Peaches was wrong and Pete didn't appear to me to be living like no monk, he didn't show any signs of settling down and he never took a girl home to meet his people. Her partiality drove us damn mad; nothing new; same way she used, when we were children, to insist that boys should not wash plate or clothes and the damn boys get so ridiculous and uppity as a result, that if rain set and nobody else was around to take the clothes off the line, they would take up everything else except the girls' panties because of some female taint that they imagine. The same taint, located somewhere between wi legs, that made it ok for us to wash the dirty plate they eat off, while they swan it about the place an jeer us. Mumsy and me had it out in the house one day; Papsi had was to intervene to prevent bloodshed, even if was only verbal bloodshed. Papsi was always a much fairer person, and was because of him the boys had to start washing plate and they own underwear, which Mumsy and then the helper used to have to wash. And a rule establish – *if yu alone at home an rain fall, tek up **all** di clothes off di line.* Now I knew that Pete and most Jacarandan man can beat the hell out of any woman when it come to cooking; is a art form they pride themselves on, so I don't know what my mother was going on about. I get a backsiding the evening she and I come to verbal blows and Papsi arbitrate, for I tell Truck, 'Yu bitch yu. Oonu can tear it off woman when it dirty but oonu can't take it off the clothesline when it clean,' and Truck tell her and she beat me. Papsi couldn't shield me from the bus' ass that time, for even he had to admit those kinds of words I tell Truck not suppose to come out of any decent young girl mouth. But I wasn't a decent young girl in those days. I was a teenager wearing a size 38 D cup brassiere and because of that I had was to learn how to defend myself with filthy words from long long time.

When my mother fretting up herself over Pete not eating properly because he not married, I not even paying her any mind because I know Pete not only can well and cook, Pete not eating because he don't know what to do with himself with him half shadow, Tram, gone.

I couldn't have known then, how short a time it would be before my mother get her wish and Pete bring a woman home, or how short a time before, night and day, my brother was cooking, fi big family too. Jackass seh di worl' nuh level. My mother imagining that these two developments mutually exclusive. She couldn't have been wronger.

It funny but not surprising how after a while Pete seem to have found an inner peace that nobody know where it really come from, but everyone silently blame it on Evangeline. Evangeline had that effect on people. She mad as hell and hatter and march hare rolled into one, but she have a way of finding the right word to preach or praying a prayer that mek yu either nervous or profoundly grateful, because is like she go into yu deepest inside and tek out the thoughts and feelings you yourself didn't even know yu was thinking or feeling, and she have a way of presenting them shameless before God like she and God is fren, and yu feel to seh yu an Him cooda did fren as well – if Him wasn't so much like Evangeline, wasn't so exacting and picky-picky, can't leave a thing alone without having to root it out and harass yu about it. I figured Pete had nothing to hide or root out after psychotherapy and hypnosis, so if Evangeline jump-up God-therapy working for him, I wished him well. After all the worst could happen would be he put on Pope mitre an dress up inna robe like Evangeline an start preach barefoot at crossroad. I wasn't sure it would be worse than him walking around empty-eyed like zombie, especially as it don't seem to do Evangeline any real harm, for underneath the madhouse look and the fly-up-inna-Spirit ways, she sane and steady as day. Mad as shad but sane as day – is only in Jacaranda yu see dat kind of perplexity, ehn?

★

When the news bus', was the second time Pete cause Mumsy to have to take extra dose of blood pressure medicine and go doctor go check her heart to see if it attack.

I tell you, Pete never dead because of Tram. Just as how Tram never dead because of man. Is pure lie people telling. I say Pete died because Jacaranda become a bloodthirsty place, where people settle dispute with knife and gun.

But maybe it's more complicated. A major part play by that monkish spirit my brother have, that Peaches talk about.

A life has to mean something. Tram made sure hers did. Have to do something for somebody, give something for somebody. Not because they need more than I do. That is just religious claptrap from people who like to patronise other people. Who is to measure need? No, give because otherwise you die inside yourself, to yourself. What is the use of a life, if it belongs to the dead? The living cry out for something more.

In the end maybe I couldn't blame Evangeline.
Or maybe I could.

My brother got married in the year after Tram husband die. And like some kind of Christ, the boy was thirty-three years old. Same age as Jesus when him crucify, an a crucify mi bredda get crucify. He was the last of us to marry except Peaches, who had no use for man in her house (though she have them out of door, and I can't say I blame her), and Evangeline, who don't count, for she find her all-sufficiency in her God.

So he bring the woman home and as her eyes light on the woman my mother start to warn, get into one set of spirit and start to warn, like some carnival version of Evangeline receiving news from the other side.

But is not no revelation, you know, is prejudice pure and simple. I have to admit. The girl ten years older than Pete, can hardly call her a girl, ehn? And worse, she had club feet, walked with a rock-and-roll limp on two platform boot shoemaker make specially for her. Behind her a string of children, seven of them in all, one behind the other like stepladder, no more than two years or a year between each one and the one before it. Seven children, seven different man. And with a reputation in Bypass, where he meet her, for lying down at any first man she meet, just like how hog wash at the first mud him ketch.

Now when I think about these things it feel like fiction. I know for sure my brother gone mad but my mother went ballistic. She put her hand on her head and she bawl, she hold her belly and she wail; was like Rachel travailing for her children, and to be comforted she would not.

Over the years my mother had learnt silence and did her best not to interfere in her children's, especially her sons' affairs, but this was not an affair, it was a marriage and as far as any of us could see, a disaster. My mother took on Pete in one long everlasting harangue, and the upshot of it was Pete burst from the house in a rage, telling Mumsy he would never return to her house if his wife was not welcome there, and from that point on he and Mumsy were estranged. I have no words to remember how my mother's heart broke.

In desperation Mumsy appealed to Evangeline. Evangeline

was troubled but philosophical. In other words, as irritating as usual. 'Mama, all I can do is pray. Pete is a big man, I cannot tell him what to do. Moreover, he is already married; what you going to do? Arrange a divorce? The most I can do is pray.'

Frustrated, my mother accused Evangeline of orchestrating, aiding and abetting the marriage. 'She come to your house, don't? All the time he was coming down here, was that vile Jezebel him was meeting with, don't? At your house too! And you call yourself a parson? You should be ashamed of yourself!'

It was a while before Evangeline could calm her down enough to listen. 'Mama, I am as taken by surprise as you are. I had no idea he was in a relationship with Maryam. When he told me he was going to marry her – yes, he did tell me, and no, it wasn't I who conducted the wedding – I think Pete sensed that if he asked me the whole family of you would malice me, so he didn't. I talked with him about it, asked him if he was sure he knew what he was doing and what the consequences would be –'

'Evangeline, stop talk fart in mi ears! Ask him if him sure about what? Sure what? Yu don't see the boy stark staring raving mad and him don't recover from Tramadol, yu don't see? Yu can ask madman if him know what him doing?'

'Mama, calm down, calm down,' Evangeline kept on uselessly for a good while. Finally, as if bent on provoking my mother, she ask one of those deadpan questions that only Evangeline can ask when she playing devil's advocate or, as she put it, God's advocate, the kind of question you don't ask my mother because it mean you think you are the only reasonable person in the room and you teaching the rest, including your mother who older than you. 'Mama, tell me truly, what do you really have against the girl?'

'Girl? What girl? Dat is not no girl, dat is a big old bubba tree ooman old enough to be the boy grandmother.'

'Not quite,' Evangeline said dryly. 'But I see. It's her age you have a problem with, then. Age is not a sin, you know, Mama.'

'Don't patronize me, Evangeline,' my mother rejoined

wrathfully. 'The woman older than Methuselah wife when it come to experience, except that Methuselah wife was decent woman, not no whore. Yu realize is seven pickni shi have fi seven man?'

'Yes.' Evangeline stood there looking troubled. Then she said, 'I agree it's not a good track record, but Mama, you don't know her story. We don't really know why this. And the fact that she married Pete might well be a sign that she has turned her back on that way of living. We have to have hope and grace, you know. God can do anything.'

'That may be so, but Him help those who help themselves.' My mother writing her own Bible, for, as Evangeline love to point out, that verse not in the one we was given. 'And Him seh yu mustn't be over-foolish, or over-wise. You don't have no pickni so you don't know how it feel. What going to happen to my one son, my beautiful son? How him going to father seven bad-begotten pickni, none of which is his?'

'I don't have no pickni, true,' Evangeline said quietly. It was a thing she had been taunted with, many a time. 'But since you have nine, you might know how Maryam feels. What it is like to hear them cry in the night because you didn't have food to give them before they went to bed, and there won't be any breakfast in the morning.'

'I have my children in fast and decent wedlock,' Seraphine retorted. 'And if I had lie down in every bush and canepiece I pass, so man and sundry can breed me, I wouldn't be calling upon anybody else to mind my bad-begotten offspring, only mi and dem father. And if no father, mi one.'

'I don't know that she called upon him, Mama. Pete chose. For his own reasons he wanted to offer his love to this woman and her children.'

'Love? Smaddy can love dat? What kind of love is dat, dat batten on a lamefoot whore with seven jacket pickni like step trailing behind her?'

'Mama, mi sure Pete have sex with more than seven woman in him lifetime.' Evangeline began to get irate. She was, after all, Seraphine's daughter, with long experience of sorrows at the mean end of her mother's skewed gender politics. When she got irate she was pure Jacarandan, no British. 'Yu calling him whore? Furthermore who tell you the children are jacket? And yu insulting God by passing remarks on the woman's foot, for is not she make herself.' She don't mention the other thing she know bugging Mumsy, the fact that the girl have no education to speak of and her son is big-big computer self-CEO with degree in IT programming.

Seraphine feel suddenly tired, tired; she sit down sudden on Evangeline sofa and hold her head. 'Evangeline, done, jus done. Mi tiad.'

Evangeline was silent for a long time, looking pensive out the window of her living room in Bypass where her mother had come to have out this confrontation. The room was not silent; it was full of the sound of Seraphine's breathing like a woman carrying a heavy load, the unspeakable weight of her rage and despair. At last her madhouse daughter spoke. 'Maybe it's the only kind there is.'

'Eh?'

'Love. You ask what kind of love it is that can batten on a lamefoot whore with seven pickni trailing behind her. I said maybe that's the only kind of love there is.'

'Yes, all that sound nice and pretty inna yu mealy-mouth and from pulpit, nuh? But this is flesh and blood, Evangeline. My flesh and blood. Bone.' My mother shouted out the last word, like somebody stab her. 'Bone!'

Her daughter was silent again, and then she said it again, as if this time it was for herself. 'Maybe it's the only kind that matters, in God's record book. Mama, I don't say I am not concerned, as you are. But for different reasons, though I know how you feel.' She saw the spark rising in Seraphine's eyes at the words 'I know how you feel', and fielded it with her own unwavering, fierce stare. 'Pete has been through a lot. Things that take you to the bedrock of things, of yourself, of who you are. He has – loved – a lot. And lost. And I think he has revised the meaning of love and what he thinks is the nature of things, in a pretty total way. I respect him for that. My real fear is whether he can carry it through, in the face of how the whole family carry on like him kill sacred beast; in the face of what people going have it to seh; in the face of how Maryam might be – him can't mek her into a image, she is still flesh and blood and human and hope and sin. And most of all in the face of how he himself might be, when the excitement of daring settle.'

Seraphine bitterly repented her visit and vowed to say nothing more in the face of what she called Evangeline's almshouse religiosity. She cut her eye and kiss her teeth; later on, without ceasing, she wept. (I know that like me, Mitch and Peaches suspected her of visiting guzzum to break up Pete's marriage, but we each kept our suspicions to ourselves, making talisman from silence: if you don't say it, it won't be true, it will go away).

★

Later when I read Pete's diary and see how Evangeline's language in this conversation match with his entry dated just before he marry Maryam, I feel sure Pete absorb self-sacrificial claptrap from Evangeline and that was one more thing I find it hard to forgive. She hurt my brother and wrong my mother too bad; I don't know if I can ever look in her face again.

And he wrestled, you know, the bouts of what seemed like lucid serenity fighting with the madness, which the serenity was only another face of.

> *Vangie says I must explore my doubts, live in them. That way I will know if, and when, I come out on the other side. 'Stop believing and start doubting.' I don't have to start doubting. Is how to stop. I am probably doing something completely mad; Maryam is as afraid as I am, worse in fact. She thinks I am using her as an experiment, that I don't really love her. Saving my own soul, so to speak. But man and woman love is two different something, I have heard. In the end, though, the passion has to speak for itself. I have to trust it, believe that behind it is something more. If only because we are both human, and what we are is yet to be discovered, but so vast, so awesome. If we both commit to this, we will be ok.*

In Evangeline's book, and Tram's whom he adored, Pete was suffering not from madness or depression but from the only sanity there was. I tell you is pure mad people in my family, is not lie Micheline telling. Is only mad people think themselves sane. *'In the end the passion has to speak for itself.'* Sound to me like the woman so full of experience she know how to mek man feel her poom-poom is the sweetest in the world, and mi fool-fool on-the-rebound bredda get caught and think him discover the wide Pacific like Cortez and his men, silent upon a peak in Darien. So him start looking behind the poom-poom for something him hoping might be there.

Might be there. Dear God I wish I could believe, had any way of believing he found that something there. Not just a wide-open cunt. I probe the diaries of my memory to see if I can remember a day when he was happy.

> *All my life I've been the master of compromise. Today I want to walk straight through to the other side, no waiting for her to come half way.*

This was dated on his wedding day. His was a strange kind of diary. It wasn't a diary that recorded things that happened. Just thoughts. Sometimes you could tell *if* something happened but not necessarily when it happened; he was more interested in wrestling with his response than with the event itself. Another thing was that it wasn't a regular diary, meaning he wrote in it not every day but only when he was unhappy or had something he needed to work out to his satisfaction. So there were no records of happy days. Or maybe it was just that he was unhappy all the time. The worst part is not knowing.

There were many records of conversations between them, or rather, of what he thought about afterwards, after the conversations.

> *We've tried to be frank with each other. Maryam has been hurt a lot. By gossip. By other women because of her limp. By men. She's very frank. About letting me know she is not sure she can really give me what we vowed to give each other in the wedding ceremony. It's a matter of trust. She's used to protecting herself by keeping men jealous, refusing to let*

any one think he has control of her. She wrote to me again yesterday. 'I've never surrendered to anyone. I'll cook your food, even wash your clothes, that don't take nothing off me. I not a suffragette. I will give you my body and be your wife. But I never surrendered to anyone. I don't know how to do that. Or if I want to. Don't say I didn't tell you.'

I tell her to keep her surrender to herself. That I'm not some imperial male conqueror coming to seize all. There's a part of everyone that belongs to oneself, and a part that can only belong to God. B used to say anything more, for a woman, is the curse of Eve, not to be tolerated [How shocked I was to see my name in his diary, like this]. *That all I want from her is this honesty, always. I don't know if it is true. I'm in this marriage in the name of surrender, and here I am telling her something that she might interpret to mean I'm giving myself the freedom to do as I like, not to be committed. To make her jealous by having other women.*

His next entry was cryptic.

And that's exactly how she has interpreted it. Our first fight. And she throws my words back in my face. I don't have another woman. What the hell.

Am I so deep-dyed a liar that I lie even to my own self, without knowing? I accuse her of holding back. 'You said you wanted only honesty!' 'Yes, but you're holding back even that too!' 'What yu mean, even that? Yu want something more?' 'What more?' 'You tell me!' I can't tell her. I don't trust, I don't trust, I don't trust.

What had happened to make him write that? Mitch and Peaches and I combed the annals of our memory for things we might have heard around those dates, that year, and came up with nothing. All we knew was that his diaries grew more and more irregular, more disjointed – to us, more confused – and that all was not well in Marital Faeryland; high ideals and a passionate poom-poom had not been enough to keep the terrors at bay. And didn't I know, who had married believing far less but maybe hoping for as much, possibly even more than Pete had?

He was tormented by self-doubt. And doubt of her. The thing that shocked me was that he didn't tell her about Tram. He told her he had never been in a committed relationship before, and I guess in a sense it was true. But not honest. He kept back the most intimate part of his secrets. In giving her those phony words of freedom, he gave himself permission not to surrender. Man! Chuups! Yu si dat ting dem call di mankind of our species? Oh Jesus.

> *Perhaps if Tram were still married, or – God Almighty – dead, I could have talked more frankly about her. But Maryam will never believe me that that is over. And perhaps I am not admitting to myself the fear that Maryam will ask for more, say let her go, open the door of that room and let the ghost out, let me inside. One love does not have to cancel another, but I am afraid Maryam thinks it must. Her jealousy and fear are too much of late. I will give her everything but that. But she doesn't trust me. She doesn't trust herself to win and keep a man's love. But it hasn't got anything to do with that, has it? One is loved because one is, not because of any skill or prowess in winning or impressing. Or what people call beauty or chastity. One is. It's the most awesome thing. I am because I am. I was made, therefore I am. Can we/I see past the rest to this incredible open space of glory?*

Yet he had an entry, on a page by itself, clean page on either side.

> *Tramadol Pointy is an extraordinarily beautiful woman.*

Then later, on another disconnected, almost blank page:

> *All of this is veiled in flesh. Can I see through the flesh to this incredible space of glory?*

The storm has swallowed spit, braced itself against the throbbing universe and come again with a vengeance. Rain is a crescendo on the roof, a thunder in the gables; the trees scream again in the renewed onslaught. Beatrice thinks suddenly, irrelevantly of the animals in the fields. For most of her life she had watched storms and hurricanes commit devastation without thinking of how cattle and donkeys and mules and horses managed in the wind and rain; then suddenly, some years ago, she found herself thinking about them and actually praying that they would be well. What a horrible thing to be a cow or a donkey or a mule in a country where people did not build barns for shelter, because there was no winter. Until now. Until the last few years, when the weather went all awry, earth's heart breaking.

B gets up from her kitchen table, limps slow and cramped to the back door and slides the latch. Her dogs Bruno and Kiss are curled warm in the closed-off wash area, their muzzles stretched out on their front paws beside their pans of water and leftover dog food. They are glad to see her. They rise quickly, untidily to their feet, orbit her, tails wagging, toenails and the pads of their paws clicking, beating on the stone floor, leaping desperately to kiss her after the long loneliness and fear of abandonment behind the closed door. She soothes them, and they thrust against her, hiding their faces from the blue flash of lightning and whimpering a little as the great thunder rolls. When it subsides she rubs their ears, faces, and goes back inside.

At the table she gazes into the heart of the third lighted candle. Rama Rama Sita Rama. Better leave that. The Lord is my Shepherd, I shall not want…

★

It soon became clear that either Pete's wife returned to her old ways, or he suspected her of doing so. The diary was bitter and self-accusing. Laden with suspicions, angers, recriminations, repentances.

> *I am so unjust to her, unjust. No wonder my family defines itself in secrets. To lay yourself open to another by telling your past, the worst of risks. I have wanted to give her everything, be everything. Instead I use it against her. She swears he was just a family friend. Trust. One learns to*

trust not the words, or even the deeds, but the heart of another.

Maryam, give me your heart.
I know, I know, you lost it, years ago. Hear it crying behind you in the night, trying to get back in. You told me.
There are other things. I cannot name.

I burn with shame for my brother the Peeping Tom, and the woman who, it seemed to me, taunted and held him firm with her past, the bait of what she had been and could still be, if she wanted. I wondered how those children lived in such a house that daily smoked on fire, but Evangeline said most of them didn't; Maryam had sent all but the youngest, the girl Avette, to live with their fathers, and they came and went at intervals.

★

Life went on among us. Peaches came down from Kingsport to show us her new baby daughter, Rose, and the following year Truck, who lived with his wife a hundred miles away in Milchester, produced twins, Jana and Khaleel. Mumsy planted trees for each of them, strong cedar saplings where the Pointy land rose after it dipped in the gully below the house. Papsi added two new rooms to make space for the increased influx of grandchildren that would visit in the summer when school was out. I watch Mumsy's face for the light that light up her eyes at the sight of new children, but the light now constantly chase by shadow, though she holding them on her lap laughing and they giving her joy. She make my blood run cold when I hear her say things like, 'Children are a arrow in the heart, grievous is the heart that have its quiver full of them' (was a woman who always love the poetry of Scripture but find it couldn't contain the weight of her griefs, so she always edit it to suit herself, like it was a vessel that can expand to fit occasion). Other times I hear her saying to herself, or the neighbour across the fence, 'When they young they tie up yu foot, when they old they tie up yu heart.' She telling the neighbour, 'Yu know, I used to think, when I first having

79

children, that I would be free of them when they grow up. Not so. It worse now, for now you have no control over what they do with theyself,' and Papsi getting irate and addressing her, because he know where all that coming from. 'Is what that yu talking, Seph? Is what that yu telling people?' Mumsy glad for the quarrel that his interruption precipitate, for now she can cuss him out, cuss the air blue to relieve her feelings, though Papsi not answering. Papsi have his own heartbreak over Pete marriage, but he not talking, and he not answering Mumsy quarrel, he only say, 'Seph, stop the noise and go inside', and kiss his teeth and walk out the yard.

★

We have grown years of silence, like barnacle pon crab back. When Pete's son was born, Seraphine could not contain her curiosity (not her love, her curiosity), and she journeyed to Kingsport to view the child. She came back saying he was jacket, not a single wrinkle in him looking like Morris or Pointy, and Pete was not a madman but a certified fool.

If Pete ever asked the question that Seraphine asked and answered for herself, it was not in his diaries, those tattered intimations of my brother's life that I pulled from flaking pages that fall apart again and close up meaning as I pull. His whole demeanour changed; all you could hear in him, both during the pregnancy and after the child's birth, was pride and joy. Was like my brother go on a far journey in search of heself, over glass mountain and briar-rose forest and be-witch sea, and come to the end of it all, where was a mirror of clear water, and look down in it and see him own face, and find him was a man. Was like him come to know the word born-again. Him write up all sorta plan, mek will, tek out education insurance, shower him wife wid all manner of gift. He called the child Davidow, after our youngest brother.

Micheline and Peaches and I were determined that a line had to be drawn. Upset about Pete marrying the wrong kind of woman was one thing, but, Mumsy, on what basis do you deny his child a place in the family just because you suspect it may not be his? I remind myself that at this time we knew nothing of what was going on between Pete and his wife because is only after he bury we find the diaries. So we welcomed the child with open arms and it was we who insisted that like all the other grandchildren whose parents lived away, in foreign or other parts of the country, he had a right to come and stay at Big House during the summer holidays. And when Mumsy screw up her face we tell her Evangeline seh so, though Evangeline was away at the time. Mumsy don't like Evangeline but she fraid of her enough to obey.

Pete sent him. He came with his sister Avette, a skinny, needy child with over-big ackee-seed eyes and a compulsion to confession. Was the only child I knew would confess easy as pie that is she tief out the food on the stove or break the new vase. Next minute she would confess again that is lie she telling on herself. To my mother, signs of a bad seed. To us, signs of a troubled child.

Davidow, our brother, was quite flattered that his eldest brother's son was named after him. Our mother was extraordinarily inventive when it came to naming; repetitions of names were not common in our family because there were always so many to go around, pulled out of our mother's imaginative repertoire like rabbits out of a hat (and we use to breed like rabbits too, so just as well). So Davidow well and feel good. Davidow junior (we soon called him Davvy for short and to avoid confusion) was tall for his age; as a teenager he became big and rawboned where Pete was fine-drawn, like a pencil sketch, with his bones elegant. If you was a fair person, you couldn't say Davvy didn't look like him. You couldn't say he looked like him either. He was just himself, a child called Davidow after his youngest uncle, bigger than his age, with open, pleasant features they say look like mine, an innocent expression, a taste for using his fists, and, like his sister, a tendency to lie, though without her urge to self-accusation or confession. More like self-preservation, for he never admitted to anything even if you caught him in the act; would stare you in the face and tell you, *Is not me, Auntie, is a likkle boy that climb over the fence jus a minute ago. See him there, see him there, running away! Hey boy, come back, come back!* Whether was a result of dreaminess, for the only definite resemblance between him

81

and Pete was this other-world dreaminess, or self-defence against the reserve he sense against him in some of the family, or him mother bad-blood that manifest in him half-sister as well (the gospel according to Mumsy), the fact was that the child could not tell a straight truth. Apart from the bland looks and the fighting and the Mister-Nobody-did-it fetish, the only other thing about him was his love of music; never see a child could shimmy or shake a leg at the sound of a rhythm so soon, before he come out of nappies. Papsi loved him and gave him a mouth organ. Boy blow that thing night and day, nearly mad wi.

Pete, under duress from Evangeline, come down one time, and him bring him wife, but they don't stay; the atmosphere stilt; Mumsy avoid talking to her daughter-in-law, who we none of us like for she suck up too much, try too hard to please, like somebody hiding something. Pete kiss him teeth and tell Evangeline him wi' come back when Mumsy grow up. Well taught by Evangeline, Peaches and Mitch tell him is him need to bend; him young and Mumsy old and set in her ways; give her time. Pete don't budge. But him send the child. He knew the child would be welcome, for even Mumsy hardened heart can't resist a child, and he want his son to have inheritance, the inheritance of family. In all the long diaries, only one reference to the fallout with his mother. *Mama, all of us black people come from the same history. Is just that some luckier than most.*

The storm is wearing itself out. Rain playing diminuendo on the rooftops now. Dogs whimpering in the washroom, scratching at the door to be let out, or in. Snails climb up against the window glass and B pushes it open three inches and throws salt down the ledge, the wall, sees the snails hook and curdle, their lemon-coloured bellies clench and cramp, as they fall backwards into the soaked earth. She tends to her dogs, soothes them in soft murmurs, opens the padlock and lets them rush out, wildly ecstatic, to do their thing in the places they have marked. She waits, looking out at the drenched, surreal bluescape, and then calls them back in. They come reluctantly, sniffing beaten grass, falling snails, soldier crabs and the blue-black night, but finally they come, and she locks them in again, after letting them mill in the confined space a little.

The blaze of seven candles in front of her making the kitchen ghostly and dance, Beatrice is thinking about joy. The obsession of joy in the diary of years, the lilt of a man becoming a father, learning himself for the first time, like an alphabet, or a new language that is coined. Among all his other stepchildren, he seemed to have adopted Avette in his heart as his own, but it was Davidow who remade the world in his eyes. Unto us a child is born. Unto us a son is given.

I guess and piece together the remaining years, the overtaking of joy by shadow; renewed quarrels; open accusation of infidelity; at last, the cruellest taunt of all.

> *To say yes it is true, is one thing. To say Davvy is not mine, is another. How she must hate me, to do this to my son. To do this to me through my son.*

And he write this the year Tram die, the year he go back in therapy, the same year he write in the diary:

> *I owe Tram something. Perhaps if she had been alive I could have talked more frankly about her. But to do so now, is like putting a lid on her, colour her dead.*

The same year his wife hack his computer and find his emails to Tram, and hell break loose.

> *We have passed the last frontiers of unbelief.*

In the last recorded quarrel she screamed at him, expletive after expletive, cursing him for monumental effrontery, his project, she said, to save her from herself. Damn you, I do not want to be saved. My self is what I have, how dare you take it from me, save it from me?

★

Evangeline calls from South Korea. She is between sessions in an anthropology conference. What is wrong over there? Who is unwell? The family shivers, afraid again of Evangeline's dark sayings. She has writhed all night in prophecy, says anguish took her left side and her hand came away with blood;

she slid off her bed unable to govern her limbs, in a state of rigor mortis, and when she asked 'Who?' no voice answered but there in her vision was Papsi, lying eyes closed, elegant, stretched out in white and black. Characteristically, she tells us none of these details, until afterwards. Wanting to spare us, in case it don't happen after all.

We tell her everyone is fine, as far as we know. We know what is going to happen now. This is Evangeline we talking about. Three days fasting and prayers begging God for mercy, or until the tide breaks.

★

The sounds of the set-up for Pete reverberate around the district.

> 'Go dung a Manuel Road, fi go bruk rockstone!
> Bruk dem one by one, gal an bway!
> Bruk dem two by two, gal an bway!
> Mash yu finger nuh cry
> Play wi dah play, gal an bway!'

Dominoes slamming loud on table tops, Davvy beating the gerreh drum for his father, mucus from tears sealing his eyes shut, Mitch, Peaches and me pouring mint tea, chocolate tea, passing out tough crackers, our faces lock in hard like wi bracing against rockstone.

On the corner by the crossroads, a lone figure, waiting. Avette waiting for Evangeline, to tell her how it happened. A fever of confession upon her. She waits till the evening, but Evangeline does not come; her plane is delayed. Snow has bound in the planes; how many days now, no plane can fly. Avette will not stay the night, the weight that she carries inside is too heavy to unload in dribbles, in repeated tellings to the unsatiated or the curious; she must lay it down in one mighty heave, once and for all, and it is Evangeline she wants to tell. In the end it is I who must relay to Evangeline the message that Avette left. I who must cry again with rage against my brother, this time for so carelessly getting himself killed.

I see the terrified young girl hold on to my brother at the

front door, *Don't go in, Daddy, don't go in.* See him put her aside gently – he would always be gentle – and go into the fateful house, leaving her holding her belly on her knees on the front step, trembling, then follow him inside. I see my brother standing mute at a doorway, his face closed and open on unspeakable things. I see him turn and walk away into the kitchen, and come back with the knife in his hand. I see my brother hold the naked man by the throat and I look into his eyes and I see himself leave him the way it left him the day he cursed me and the day he told his mother never again, never would he come back to her house, where his wife was not welcome, and then I see his eyes open wide and himself come back to himself again. I see himself return, I see him go back inside himself and find Pete, not Pete the stranger who cursed but Pete the brother I knew, and I see when my brother let his arm fall with the knife and walk away. I see like on Youtube when the man eye narrow and he creep up behind Pete and jump him and grab his knife arm hanging loose like a man's manship after the act of love. I see the frantic girl run out in the street screaming and flagging at car and taxi but no-one stopping but driving on in fear, for they see the long blood travelling out the door up the street, for is only blood, not water, that travel upward, along artery and vein while a person standing up, blood walking up the street to the JP house. I see the child running back inside to call 119 and then outside again to beg car and taxi for mercy, then at last kneeling by the big man she has wrapped in a sheet to stanch the blood, kneeling helplessly to stanch the blood, holding his hands now growing cold in her small fingers, saying the Our Father with him, as we forgive our debtors, tell Davvy not to fight for me, don't forget, not to fight for me, for Thine is the kingdom for Thine is the kingdom, tell Mama, tell Mama, and the police coming at last too late too late to see the beginning where the woman run out the back door wrapped in the soiled burning sheet or the afterwards when the man walk out and go to the station with him testimony of self-defence, and is we see the bitter after-afterwards in the courtroom when the woman say she was not there, when the woman say is business-feud, for the man work in Pete office and Pete plan meeting to accuse him of tiefing company goods but she was not there and she don't see what happen, and the neighbours keep silent for they fraid for they life, though they see the woman running out wrapped in the guilty sheet, and Avette not there to say is not so. Avette not there to say is not so. Oh God Almighty, Avette not there to say is not so.

★

This storm does not know how to make up its mind. Wind and rain rising again, lightning and thunder, unweary, start again criss-crossing the sky as if searching for a way out of they cycle, a unlocking. Is Beatrice beginning to think the storm following her up and down, is not pathetic fallacy.

Years she vex with them all. With Mumsy for not letting Pete go; with Pete for being too noble and too stupid and too wrong; with Evangeline, who too holy to cry, Evangeline who always thinking God going put life first, when life and death is all the same to Him; with Micheline who think a person can just mek fable and forget; with herself for having them up in her heart all these years, for vexing with them all and not letting any of them go. She find she can't even vex with the woman who get him killed, for she still don't understand anything about what really happen or how this woman mind work. But she hate her still, and she hate the woman bad-seed pickni still.

She say to herself is many reasons, all of them bound up in somebody fault, why Pete die young. But maybe the real reason is as simple as the sound Cousin Jacob's head made hitting the sidewalk when he fell off the truck and died, leaving Tram without a father and my foolish brother at the age of six, with the misguided idea that he could fill that gap or heal that wound.

The simple thing is, my brother died because he was a thin man. He didn't have enough to eat in how long; no body fat to protect him from the knife. The knife slide so slick, so smooth, from mi brother ribs to him heart.

At the postmortem my two remaining brothers run. So I

stand up in their stead. I brace my breast the way I always brace it to face down the world and I say yes, this is my brother, and that satisfy the pathologist fi cut him again, as if the murderer's knife was not enough. The pathologist shout with vex when I turn my face away. As if by shouting he could wrench my face in the right direction, towards the knife in his hand. A knife so sharp its blade was blue.

But they say funerals are for the living. They say that at funerals, the guilty weep. At my brother's funeral, is nuff people weep. So much weeping that it bring thunder and lightning down from the sky, and when it over, a big lake form that cover the grave, the cemetery and the road. The Parish Council build a detour road for pedestrian and vehicular traffic. It still there, if you go and look. Intersection of Seaview and Main Drive, leading up to where the returning residents live. In the town of Bypass, because everybody pass wi by.

From a distance, the lake of eyewaters look solid and white as a sheet of salt. Up close, it crystal clear. You can see your face in it. If you kneel down and peer over the edge, your face grow big and fill up the space, the way a picture fill the frame when the camera pan. If a tree shiver or a wind pass by, your face break up and break away.

The lake skilful, like a camera.

In this, it no different from any other body of water. What make it different is that, apart from faces, no living thing grow there. Like the Dead Sea, it too salt. Small children try swimming in it, but they soon give up. The water current thick, it don't move, and the children feel a dread knocking, knocking gainst their limbs, and they come out with their eyes wide open and staring, and their eyelashes shock and cake with silver.

One time, I try to cross over from the concrete road to the lake, to visit my brother in him underwater grave. I park my car a little short of the lake. A taxi driver with a car full of passenger cross over from his side of the road and ram my car. The car so broken that my insurance almost call it a write-off. My brothers, my sisters, my mother, look at each other dumb when this happen; nobody say a word. But I could see the words of fear in they eyes: 'Is a sign.' Since then, seven years this day, no one visit my brother. A sign of what? That my brother does not want to be visited? Or that the murdered do not rest in their graves? Or that there is no washing away guilt after death – that if you sin against someone, after his death is just the judgement?

I dream of conversations with my brother. Conversations I do not have, because I fraid for him to come into the room. Is why I always burning candle, candle.

Shortly after my brother pass, before the wake, I see him in his funeral clothes, the same black bow-tie and pants, white shirt, that we bury him in. Same clothes that Evangeline vision him in before it happen. He had something to say. Him come towards me with the quick rush to intimacy that was how him usually walk. Pete was always the touch-feely one among us, him like to come up close and touch you with him finger tips when him speaking, like him need to get your full attention. Don't know how him keep company with Shame-a-Macka-Touch-Me-Not Tramadol, yet him always like to come up close, and touch.

But this time he begin to speak before he get close to me, as if what he have to say was forcing itself out in a rush, or he was afraid I would run away instead of listening, or something was going pull him away before he have the time to finish speaking.

'I want you do something for me,' he said. 'I have something I asking you to do for me.'

'Retro me, Sathanas!' I bawl out a Evangeline chant, to ward off the dead.

The darkness erupt, in shards. When they clear, my brother not there, and I staring at the day breaking through the window. Is only God know how many messages of regret I send, through angel, through Holy Ghost, through the Son. I even call for Evangeline, but no answer come back. Who returns from the world of the dead? Are what we see chimera? Evangeline, when she was little, cried because she saw Miss Louise in a blue suit, flitting in and out of childhood rooms, playing with her the way she did before she was dead, so I used to be afraid and don't want to be alone in the house. The long processions of slave men and women with bundles on their heads my mother see walking in the river singing, 'Swing low, sweet chariot' many mornings when she stand in our yard watching the river come back to life in the mists below, two centuries after slavery's end. Granpa Butty stealing my brother Truck in broad daylight, a mash-up mash-up little man with the wind blowing through his clothes, rising from a lump in the ground. Samuel the prophet at Endor by special dispensation saying tomorrow o king, your time comes to an end; set your house in order.

All of that is chimera, or forcefield of desire?

My mother carried nine children in her womb and delivered every one of them awake. She convinced that nobody is born by themselves, and she never reconcile to the fact that people die alone. I see her sitting there on the front step rocking herself, rocking herself when she hear that Pete gone. 'If only one of us was there (where my brother, her son, lay bleeding on the floor, waiting for the ambulance that never came) to say a little prayer for him. A Our Father.' I rock her, I say, 'Mumsy, yu feget. Pete awright, it awright, he went in a good way. Don't Avette tell yu how it go? Is she seh the Our Father with him. Yu know he went in a good way, in spite of everything.'

What does even any mother know of the long passage down the womb to the bright air on a person's face? How long that journey take, and how alone? When we deading, is it a repeat of the birth-journey that we all forget, except that this time around we carry back memories? Don't make any sense ask these questions from this side of the river. The passage back through the womb of time shroud in silence. Even if the dying see the whole journey while they going, who ever return to tell us what it really like?

Is the fear of that loneliness give us premonition and make us sing with the dead.

But I know what my brother want me to do for him. I quarrelling with him for obsessing with guilt over Tram, but where Pete is concerned, I have been guilty all my life. My brother wanted justice. He knew the world didn't give him justice but he wanted us to give it to him. He wanted me to plead his cause with my mother, and he wanted me to understand. The first wasn't necessary, never need to ask Seraphine to do what her mother's heart already mek her do, and the other I too angry and grieve to do. Though is Vangie is the one who usually see spirit, I am the one he visit, because I am the one don't forgive him. Thirteen years.

It is either the long keening of the wind after the rain or it is Beatrice weeping. But the sound is changing now. On her knees on the hard kitchen floor, all of her heaves with the long, awful gusts, the sounds of a child with croup suffocating, that dredge themselves up out of deep clots inside her. Behind her, the Home Sweet Home lamp she knows now she has lighted for Pete is surrounded by the eleven lesser lights she has lighted for Mumsy, Papsi, Gramps, Granma Morris and Granma Pointy, Mitch, Peaches, Truck, Davidow, Evangeline, Vicki, and she, the candles of atonement, of encirclement for the departed and the faintly living, the dumb, the blind, the deaf and the lame who walk, stumbling.

III

BIRTH

The child born on an airplane was difficult from the start, and her whole life was taken as an omen.

She emerged into the troposphere exactly at 13.00 hours, 35,000 feet above land. The pilot touched down at Santa Fe. The plane was en route to Jacaranda, Caribbean. Emergency landing. At the hospital in Santa Fe mother and child were pronounced well, and came home to Jacaranda aboard the next BA flight with cyberkisses and champagne.

It was a lucky but not an easy birth. The mother, finding herself thrust up against the bulkhead next to first class, her legs wide open over the head of the male doctor who was mercifully travelling on the same flight and who was now peering diligently into her nether regions and urging, 'Push!' while passengers chittered, twittered, stood, or craned to see, and flight attendants shouted over the intercom, 'Passengers please, please calm down, we are asking you please to sit, stay in your seats, that is the best way you can assist this woman, please, please, don't come forward, she needs air, everything is going to be fine, we have a doctor attending her now, there is no danger to her or her baby, please, once again, we are asking you to sit down' – they themselves, however, doing plenty of craning and crowding – the mother, I am saying, finding herself thrust up against all this, was so overcome with panic and shame that she, Seraphine, opened her lungs and bawled out a string of bad words, the tone if not the sense of which was well understood by all. Frightened at the power and vigour of her curses, the flight attendants staggered backwards and began speaking in muffled tones. Some passengers laughed. Others, mainly women, cringed, cursed, threatened or exhorted the multitude, hiding their children's faces against their thighs. 'Yu never see baby born yet? What yu carrying on so for, what yu gawping at the woman for? Yu see any excitement here? What you all think? You men don't think you had anything to do with it?' a woman in a large turban, flushed with excitable wrath, accused her male companion.

'But Rita, how I come to have anything to do with it? I don't know the woman?' the man exclaimed, timid and exasperated all together.

He made a mistake. Several other women joined the fray and began lambasting him for pretending to be a fool.

'Push!' the doctor urged, encouraging. 'Push now, hard as you can. It's coming! It's coming!'

It is said that so prolific, inventive and x-rated became my mother's curses as the baby's head peaked that the air in the cabin blushed blue, and the flight attendants had to give extra oxygen.

In the end, Seraphine simply wept. As she would do again many years thereafter.

It was her first child.

The baby flew out at the moment Seraphine grabbed the doctor's face and tore it in two, exposing his gums, his teeth and the cartilage under his nose so that when they landed he too had to be rushed to the hospital to be stitched up again, the stitching done imperfectly so that ever afterwards, when called to any delivery bed, he wore a sinister and feral grin, and guarded his face with his hands.

The child came out completely encased in the amniotic sac; not a caul over her face but her entire length wrapped in jelly like an onion in its netted bag. She was exactly seven weeks premature, lay easily in the palm of one of her mother's hands, and weighed three pounds, two and a half ounces.

Everything on her was perfect. Follow-up care at hospital in Jacaranda found no ill-effects or intimations of future trouble from the fact that she had started travelling from before birth and arrived too soon.

They called her Evangeline. In the aftermath of giving birth in front of strangers between earth and air, Seraphine remembered only the joy of the child's perfection and forgave her husband, John Morris, his depredations on her person for which she had cursed him on the plane. She allowed him enough subsequent liberties that seven more children were born in the thirteen years following their spectacular daughter's eruption into the world.

But that belongs to another story.

Inevitably, legend affixed to the child, and this was the beginning of her troubles.

The first sign was when the naïve mother, barely nineteen years old and unlearned in the politics of belonging, went to register the birth and was told by the Registrar General that she could not, because the child had not certifiably been born in Jacarandan airspace.

No need to go into the details of the controversies that ensued. Suffice it to say that Human Rights Watch took up the case on Seraphine's behalf, and the outcome was that Evangeline Morris became registered as a British citizen as it was proven by aircraft records that she emerged from between her mother's legs in the minute before the plane left international airspace, which meant that she belonged to the country of the airline. If she had been born in the airspace over Santa Fe she would have been an American citizen. It seemed that there was never at any point any probability of her being born Jacarandan, since the aircraft was nowhere near Jacaranda when my sister entered the world.

In the end, because John Morris insisted that no child of his was going to be registered a foreigner and it be left there, Evangeline was also made a Jacarandan citizen by descent. This took a long and roundabout time as, first, Seraphine had to produce evidence of the child's place of birth. Since this application ran parallel with the British and American investigations, the British birth certificate was not yet issued and so Seraphine had to use the old-fashioned way of proving such things, which was to get reputable witnesses to certify that the baby had indeed been born in a certain place – in this case, an airplane in flight. This would appear on the Jacarandan birth certificate as 'Place of Birth: In the Air. Country of Birth: Unknown.' Luckily, the British birth certificate came through first and the information on it was copied onto the Jacarandan certificate. The Jacarandan document took seven months to process, from the moment of the child's registration as British, to the day she reached nine months old. That day, the beginning of her ninth month, also registered the first of the omens that enmeshed my sister's life from her birth to the grave.

Seraphine had an aunt, Rita, who was a traveller by trade. She it was, who had caused Seraphine to be in flight on the day of Evangeline's birth, having invited Seraphine to go with her to visit another relative in Wiltshire, England, and having overstayed both her time and her welcome in Wiltshire for an entire week, while the pregnancy grew. In Jacaranda, where she had a fourteen-room house in the cool hills above Bypass, the town near where Seraphine was born, Rita was known as a returning resident, even though it was more than fifteen years since she had come back from abroad to settle again in the country of her birth.

Fuming, and cursing as she had taught her niece to do, Rita spearheaded the registration-by-descent effort by daily bombarding the radio call-in shows, which served de facto as the high court of the Jacarandan poor, staging one-woman demonstrations in front of television stations, and firing off letters to newspaper editors on the side.

'It is just like those damn-fool pissing-tail galpicknis they have as Customs officers at the airport, don't know their ass from bull foot. You know how many times I come out of immigration, no problem, and as I get to Customs these stupid girls are refusing to let me through the Customs line because I refuse to tell them how long I staying in my own country?' Rita cursed, mistress as ever of irrelevant narration. 'I tell them you cannot ask me that, I am coming home to my country and I can stay as long as I like; furthermore the immigration officer did not ask me that, and it is his job to ask such questions. Why yu don't ask me what I have in the bags, or look to see if I carrying any contraband? That is your job. And the idiots proceed to tell me how the law says they can ask me any question they want, and how I am illiterate yet I call myself

Nurse Practitioner on the immigration form. That is when you know they vex with you for being able to go abroad when they can't; is pure envy. One day I hold up the line and refuse to move till they call airport police and the police let me through. I show them a Jacarandan passport; what they asking me how long I staying for?'

'But, Aunt Rita, what that have to do with the baby registration case?' Seraphine exclaimed, feeling that Rita's curses and illogical reasonings would do her case more harm than good. She would not have been surprised if the Registrar General's office held up the papers that were the baby's by right, just to spite Rita. (This was the same Rita who had accused her travelling companion on the plane of being a man and therefore responsible for Seraphine's suffering in childbirth).

'What it have to do with it? It have plenty. Same way they make it difficult for you to come back into your own country, now they denying the child her birthright. And you know what vex me most of all? I reach back in Miami airport and show mi green card and the American man tell mi, "Welcome home, Miss Morris." In stranger country, they welcoming mi, and my own people dissing mi. It hurt yu know. It hurt bad. Why wi quarrelling with white people to tek our pickni, ehn? Her mother not Jacarandan? Don't by law that mek her Jacarandan too?'

On the day Evangeline became a dual citizen and attained nine months old, Seraphine took her for her routine check-up at the obstetrics clinic.

She (that is, Seraphine) returned very disturbed.

When the nurse put the child on the scale to be weighed, Evangeline did not tip the scale and her weight did not register. Six times the nurse put the child on the scale and her weight did not register. Since from the moment Seraphine and her daughter entered the clinic people had started craning, whispering or exclaiming out loud, 'Nuh di aeroplane baby dat? Is di aeroplane baby dat!', and some accosted the mother to praise, admire, ceitful or prophesy, all eyes were already focused on Evangeline, and this strange occurrence understandably became a major sign in the eyes of onlookers. Prophecies flew, pronouncements multiplied, a warner woman wet herself, right there on the spot, and it was said that on the nurse's sixth attempt, a patoo, an owl, flew in the air in the broad daylight above the clinic.

In a rage Seraphine took her child and fled the clinic, cursing as she had done at the birth, and sworn never again to do, for she did not like to think that the spirit of Rita possessed her.

It happened that, for unknown reasons, apart from the Jacarandan warner woman, an American psychic was present in the clinic when this event took place, and so was a local newspaper reporter, on a particularly dry day for news, on the prowl for a scoop. He had been sent out by his editor to find something to lead the next day's edition. So it was that my sister appeared again in the news, (reappearing yet again seven years later in cyberspace via Youtube, Twitter, LinkedIn and Facebook when another child burst out on a plane and my sister's pioneering journey as the first one was recalled). Seraphine saw her daughter spread out in all the local media by tributary via the newspaperman's scoop; and in the *American Journal of Psychics* via the tourist psychic's article, in which she testified to having sensed an intense agglomeration of energy particles surrounding my sister at the moment the nurse lifted her towards the scale. This burst of energy, the psychic said, intensified to the nth degree until there was a flash of white light and the child floated out of gravity, as though intervening arms had lifted her away from earth, neutralizing the nurse's mass. The child lay in a sac of white light, and could not be touched by anything attached to land or solid matter. As a Jacarandan woman translated later, 'the child leave-eart'.

The clinic, annoyed, said the scale had jammed (as scales sometimes do) and been replaced, which explained why the next child to be weighed had no problems at all. This became a forgotten footnote in the annals of my sister's pilgrimage.

Seraphine was an intelligent woman. She was well aware that if her daughter was to lead a normal life, she would either have to be sent away, far from where she was known, or people would have to forget. But she knew the unlikelihood of the latter in a small village, and was convinced that her own death from despair would attend the former in no time. Since she could not bear to part with her child, even to any of the host of relatives in Miami, Orlando, New Jersey, New York, Los Angeles, Maryland, Connecticut, Wiltshire, Leeds, Birmingham, London, Buckinghamshire, Toronto, Montreal, British Columbia, Hamburg, Frankfurt, Madrid, Qatar, Senegal, Morocco, Jerusalem who were able (and some willing) to take her, Seraphine decided on a series of compromises to keep Evangeline safe, at the centre of which was a bargain with God.

Not in her wildest dreams could she have imagined the result of this course of action.

At the time all of this happened, Seraphine was pregnant again, and horribly plagued with morning sickness which could not be helped by tough crackers or mint tea or thyme tea or ginger root or what a cousin from America prescribed – egg. This sapped her energy, and before she could implement any of the compromises she had decided on, the great earthquake of '95 happened. It shook to its foundations the humble two room in which John and Seraphine lived, but left it standing, except for some broken rafters out of which fell, upon the dining table exactly in the centre of the room, a teaspoon which appeared to Seraphine to be made of beaten gold. The house had belonged to generations of Seraphine's family, the Pointys, one of whom, Jonathan Sebastien Pointy, had gone away for many years to work on the Panama Canal, in Panama, where it was said they had gold. The spoon may just have been of copper, which in the district was plentiful. But Jonathan Sebastien Pointy had worked on the Panama Canal, and the spoon, hidden away how long, was not discovered until the earthquake, which also happened to be in the month of Evangeline's birthday. In that month she was one year old.

Everything seemed to line up too neatly to speak of copper rather than gold.

Seraphine fed the child with the golden spoon.

It was at this moment that she was finally convinced that her daughter was indeed a special child.

Driven with a flash of fear because of the earthquake, she decided to put off the protection rituals no longer. She hastened to gather talismans around her child.

Her first action was to take the child to the district Baptist church, to be blessed by the finger of God. There were other churches to which she could have gone, but Seraphine took the child to the Baptist church for a reason. She was herself Seventh Day Adventist, but she had not been to church in how long, for she had backslidden and become pregnant with Evangeline before she was quite married. She did not want to have to answer questions, or confess, or be pressured back into the fold before she felt she was ready. Furthermore, the Seventh Day Adventist Church was over two miles away. Nearer to her house than the Baptist church were the churches of the Methodists, which she did not like because she found the singing 'too dead'; and of the Church of God, which she did not like because its devotees flew in the Spirit and spoke in outlandish tongues. For a Seventh Day Adventist, the Baptists were a sober compromise because Baptist singing was neither dead nor overdone but rather quite melodious, almost Adventist. Moreover, Seraphine knew of no scandals involving the Baptist deacons.

But Seraphine was in for a surprise. When the moment came to pray for the child, after all the other rituals were done, the Baptist minister, not known for flights of fancy, took the child in his arms and holding it high above the altar, began to say strange things. 'And this child of humble beginnings, as yet unknown in the world, shall wear purple and be fed with gold, and come before kings, and in the end of her days, shall stand before the face of the great King. In the name of the Father, and of the Son, and of the Holy Ghost, Amen.'

The minister spoke in the metaphoric and exalted manner of his kind, purveyors of the King James Bible and the tradition of country villages used to the ways of ghosts, warners and revivalists, an almost ridiculously ambitious people never satisfied with small, or here, or any part of their lot in life, but always worrying at invisible chains and hoeing down the ridges of their island to push their boats out to sea;

people who translated their own deaths into imageries of flame, winged chariots and the horsemanship of God. Every one of them, no matter how irreligious or wicked, was sure they would be caught up at the last trump, and would see Jesus. This was a language to which Seraphine was used. Even so, she received the minister's words not as a hoped-for blessing but as a confirmation of destiny already ordained, for who but the tongue of God could have revealed to the minister what she herself had told to no one, that her child had eaten from a golden spoon?

And the district, perversely, because the child was already marked from birth, likewise chose to receive the minister's words not as mere metaphor but as either a major prophecy or something Seraphine had bribed him to say. Some praised, some ceitfulled, others mocked.

'A God-bless pickni, yu nuh see it? Parson prophesy.'

'Prophesy it. Yes.'

'Oh yes.'

'Feed on gold? A wha shi a try fi seh, har pickni a royalty? Si ya ma, dishtowel tun tablecloth. Jus because har pickni born up inna sky, har chest start climb out of her frock?'

'Stand before king? Which king? Afta no king nuh deh again. Only one dibby-dibby likkle queen.'

'Parson nuh know what him do. Anything name Pointy – show off! Is now Seraphine foot going can't touch grung! Heh hey!'

Seraphine's second step was to finally bury the baby's navel string, kept preserved in the jar in which the Santa Fe hospital had given it to her. She could not explain to herself why she had not yet planted it, as the custom was, but now, after the christening, she felt she had been given a sign that the time was right, and so she chose out a strong breadfruit sapling that was growing near the outside kitchen below the house, dug the hole deep with her own hands, and deposited there the cord that had bound her daughter close to her. The child would grow with the tree and, being planted, would never leave her place; if she travelled, she would return again to the good earth and the people that nourished her. In this way Seraphine

101

reconciled the prophecy of walking with kings and keeping Evangeline safe at home.

Finally, Seraphine decided never to tell the child that she was a British citizen. She swore her husband and her relatives to secrecy, despite Rita's loud and contradictory animadversions on the subject. 'That don't make any sense, Ser. First of all your husband is a man can't keep him mouth shut, him go boast and tell-all as soon as him friends dem get a shot of rum into him, in fact as soon as him smell the rum shop, for yu know him head cannot hold a thimbleful of liquor; as soon as him get it him start lct out secret like floodgate open. And second of all, why yu depriving the child of her birthright? Yu know if a time going come when Jacaranda sink under the sea and all o wi go haffi run? That time she going need her foreign birth certificate.'

'You lef my husband alone, Auntie Rita,' Seraphine cried. 'And when that time come fi Jacaranda sink, is time enough.'

'Ungrateful wretch!' Rita was incensed at this temerity.

'Leave my husband and my pickni alone!' Seraphine cried again, and it was typical of the events that surrounded Evangeline that, though Rita never divulged Seraphine's secret, the quarrel loomed large, became a major Rubicon between the two women, and they did not speak to each other again for twenty years.

★

No-one knew what the bargain was that Seraphine had made with God.

★

For the next five years of her childhood, my sister did no extraordinary feats and displayed no particularly unusual proclivities. She was a normal child who played normally, laughed and cried normally, and gave normal amounts of trouble. She was very bright, starting big school early and skipping several grades so that by the time she was eight she had finished big school and was being groomed to enter high school the coming summer. But this simply confirmed that she was a Pointy: our family was noted for extremes of intellect as for extremes of everything else. The Pointy side was very bright and likely to produce geniuses. The Morris side was uncommonly dunce and likely to produce fool-fools. None of us seemed to have struck a happy medium; the two sides of our DNA ran in parallel lines without true meeting or compromise, like an ancient wound that would not suture. Our father, John Morris, had finished elementary school unable to read or write anything but his name (although, to be fair to him, if truth were told, his grandfather had hardly ever let him darken the school door). Seraphine, on the other hand, in her time had been known as a star. (None of this explains why John's children, dunce and bright alike, adored him beyond measure and cleaved to him like love bush, but looked at their intelligent mother out of the corners of their eyes, faces slanted away like culprits weighing whether to sidle or run.)

During this time Beatrice, Pete, and I, Micheline, were born. Truck, Peaches, Vicki and Davidow came later, after a gap long enough to make us three think of them as 'the younger set'. John was prospering in his job as a barber with a shop in Bypass, and the modest two room had morphed into six, with running water in the outside kitchen and bathroom. By this time Grampa and Granma Pointy had come to live in the same yard so John and Seraphine could keep an eye on them. The children had an intensely happy childhood romping together and lapping up excess affection, with the intensity with which only children can be happy, until the time came for Evangeline to go to high school. She was sent away to live with Granma Miss Crish (short for Christiana) Morris in Tekmihoe, two miles from the town of Recess where the high school was. John and Seraphine made the decision to send Evangeline to Miss Crish for two reasons. One was that Granma was living alone after Grampa Butty died and John was worried about her. Having company in the house would be good for her and at the same time Granma was not so old or feeble that she couldn't manage a sprightly eight-year-old who could do most things for herself with just a little guidance. The other was that despite John's improved fortunes, with five children to clothe and feed it was not easy to find daily bus-fare and lunch-money, along with all the other expenses of high school, and Evangeline's staying with Granma would lessen the burden considerably, since the proximity of school to Tekmihoe cut the bus fare in exactly half.

So Evangeline left us in the summer of '02.

And so (though we didn't know it then) my sister's real life began.

★

We grew used to seeing our sister only in the holidays.

★

If anyone noticed that Evangeline was growing stranger and stranger, it was Seraphine. She didn't say anything to anyone, for fear of alerting them to what they might not have seen. To anyone who wasn't looking closely, the child was merely becoming moody, precociously entering adolescence as she had entered the world and school – too early. To a mother like Seraphine, who had expended countless hours watching for signs and 'pondering these things in her heart', the signs were alarming. The best way she could describe it was to say the child was becoming an old woman. Not becoming *like* an old woman, but literally *becoming* an old woman in front of her eyes. Evangeline had no interest in playing, shunned the company of her siblings, spent the long daylight hours under the house bottom by herself, watching ants or sorting herbs, when everyone else was whooping down the river or climbing trees, stoning mangoes, wasting guinep and hog plum, and pelting dogs who climbed ignominiously on each other in the road to breed.

Sorting herbs. Stuff she walked along the riverbank gathering in the cool mornings when, unlike the other children, she didn't have to be waked and the only other purveyors of the river were the ancient slave women my mother saw carrying washpans on their heads through the river-course, skirts hoisted up and voices hide-and-seeking with the whine of water over stones.

All the old-time bush that people's great granny used to make tea and remedy for the aches and pains of body and soul – for they didn't believe in doctor nor could they afford him, and parson they did not always trust – was what Evangeline walked along the river-course diligently gathering. Jackana. John Charles. Jubbawahrin. Wild baasli. Soursop leaf. Lime leaf. Leaf of life. Sinkle bible, what in Kingsport and foreign places they call aloe vera. Duppy soursop – on internet they call it noni. Senna leaf, senna pod. Dandelion seed. Bizzi. Abbé seed. Seraphine had not realized how much of these things still grew along the river and its environs where once, long ago, a flourishing second village had been, until the people took up and moved away to where it was nearer standpipes, running water and shops. Left wild and forgotten, this natural herbarium flourished full view, yet remained unseen until Seraphine's daughter came from her grandmother's house from July to September and plucked them in careful sheaves.

The girl would sit under the house sorting her green trove into piles, then she would take out her chemistry kit and perform strange experiments upon them. Very often she wanted to boil the stuff in the kitchen, and though a part of Seraphine was intrigued and felt a certain sympathy for the girl's curiosity, her blood ran cold at the sight of a ten-year-old, stooped down like a woman seven times her age, poking through ancient medicines as if she was an obeah woman, and so she said firmly, no, you cannot bring those things into my kitchen. Being a Pointy, Seraphine was ruled by heart rather than head. Her head told her these might be the signs of a budding physician of great fame, maybe the child would go to university, qualify as a doctor and later discover some marvellous medicine, like a cure for cancer, that would pave the way into kings' palaces and the corridors of the great, as the Baptist minister had prophesied. But Evangeline's activities sent cold bumps shooting up Seraphine's arms and gave her a strange feeling of weakness, which she interpreted as signals of the devil at work, and Seraphine went with her heart. So Evangeline built a fire between four river stones in the yard and cooked her concoctions there in an empty paint tin, until her mother put a stop to that too. Without protest, the girl contented herself with drying her herbs in the sun and rolling them into brown paper to put in her satchel to take back with her to Tekmihoe at the end of the holidays.

Seraphine then forbade her going by the river, thinking that the slave duppies that processioned there were playing with her daughter. Evangeline found herbs lavishly scattered elsewhere on the land, and went on collecting. And always, under the house, this sorting, sorting, sorting, the chemistry kit, and scribbles in a binder notebook.

It seemed to Seraphine that the child's face wizened a little by the hour and her back bent over lower and lower each day. She did not know how to accost Granma Miss Crish about what was happening to the child or whether she, Miss Crish, had anything to do with it. Was she feeding the child old wives' tales about bush bath and all of that outdated, superstitious nonsense? She didn't know how to ask all of this without causing offence to her irascible mother-in-law, especially as there was no evidence that the child's untoward holiday occupations interfered with her progress in school. She came consistently at the top of her class and already her teachers were talking about grooming her to be the '16 Jacaranda Scholar. But the child had no interest in anything outside of school except this gathering of bush-bush, and indeed Seraphine never saw her read a book all the time she was at home, this child who used to devour a book a day and cried with bared teeth if Ketlyn – the next door neighbour's daughter who went to high school two years before she did and brought books for her from the public library near the school – if Ketlyn forgot to change her library book so she could start a new read.

When Seraphine questioned her she just smiled, as if congratulating herself and always gave the same answer.

'Who teach you about all this bush-bush, Vangie?'

'Nobody, Mummy. I just think about it for myself.'

'But why? Is yu granny yu see using them?'

'Not really, Mummy. They have medicine in them, Mummy.'

'That's what they teach yu in chemistry class?'

'No, Mummy. Ah checking these out.'

'Vangie, tell me the truth. Your grandmother carry you anywhere?"

The child gave her mother an old-fashioned, grown-up look out of the corner of her eyes, fully well understanding the meaning of the veiled question, buttoned her lips, and would say no more.

Seraphine began to make her visits to her daughter in Tekmihoe more frequent, and to scrutinize like a detective what was going on. She didn't find anything. Evangeline was with her grandmother much as she had been as a younger child at home: quiet, reasonably obedient, seemingly content – and it was clear her grandmother adored her. The third time Seraphine came down to prowl around, Miss Crish tackled her.

'So what yu expecting to find? Why yu following following up the child?'

'Ehn?' Seraphine opened her eyes wide in pretended innocence. 'What yu mean, Mama Morris?'

'Yu tink I don't notice how all of a sudden yu start coming down here almost every week? Or how yu poking into mi tings when mi not looking, and watching the child like green lizard pon tree?'

'Mama Morris, mi nuh know wha yu talking bout. Mi not watching, mi jus want to mek sure Evangeline awright and not giving you too much trouble or stress. Naturally, mi mus concern, yu is mi madda and shi is mi daughter. Both of you –'

'Girl, don't ceitful pon mi, yu hear?' Miss Crish raised her cane imperiously, as if to strike, and Seraphine found herself doing a dance sideways from the old lady's arm.

'If yu want to know something, come straight, don't badda wid dat under-bottom nastiness wid mi, yu hear. Icilyn don't grow yu so. That is not how Icilyn grow yu.'

'Well, since you ask mi,' Seraphine flared. 'I want to know why the child looking like old lady and cooking up all sort of nastiness like shi planning to become obeah woman.'

'What nastiness? Yu see her using anything yu don't use? Yu don't keep bizzi? Yu don't drink bassli?'

'Yes, Mama Morris, but nuh so. Vangeline not just using or drinking them in the normal way, a little bizzi here for antidote or a little leaf-of-life there for fresh cold. Shi mekking soup wid dem, all some bush I never even remember exist… And Mama, she just ten years old. Where yu ever see young people interested in that sort of thing? Dem don't drink bush tea – as far as dem concern is back-o-wall business dat. So how come Evangel…?'

Miss Crish rapped on the floor with her cane, a strangely frightening sound. Her lower face rolled up towards her forehead, like cardboard crushed between two hands, and her eyes retreated to the backs of their sockets. For a moment she had an uncanny resemblance to Evangeline when the child was sorting bush; it was as though the child was looking out through the old woman's face, or vice versa. Seraphine went dumb with shock.

'Lissen to mi good.' Miss Crish glared into her daughter-in-law's eyes. 'Lissen to mi good, Seraphine. Stop your foolishniss. Nothing do the child. She eat, sleep healthy. Yu here and you see for yourself. She read her book, do her schoolwork. From yu come here yu don't see her with no herbs. If is a hobby she do it in her time. Be not deceived. This child yu worrying yourself up over, she go walk with president, prime minister and king. You don't worry yourself.'

Seraphine struggled to recall whether Miss Crish knew the story of the Baptist minister's prophecy or whether this was a new, totally original version of the prophesy, and could not. It was enough to strike her dumb again, this time for good. And she had to admit that when the child was by Granny Miss Crish she seemed completely different; in her face and gait she was ten years old again.

Seraphine, still vaguely troubled, eased down on her visits. She did broach the subject of bringing Evangeline home, but John was so adamantly against it that she backed down for fear of precipitating what bade fair to become the irreconcilable quarrel of their marriage. Indeed she was not totally convinced that this would have been a good option, and not only because of the money. The strain of the double distance and three buses to school would have been considerable for the child, and would no doubt have adversely affected her spectacular grades.

The next summer when Evangeline went home, she was reading again. Voraciously. But what she was reading was not the story books she had loved but a King James Bible almost as big as she was, for Evangeline was a small statured child. Now, as a devout woman who made her children read Bible on Friday nights at the start of the Sabbath and saw to it that they refrained from play, walked hush-puppy and talked only softly in the yard until sundown the next day (unless they were going to church, where the regime was more or less the same), Seraphine would normally have been delighted at any show of uncoerced devotion in her children. But this was Evangeline, and the course of her devotion took a peculiarly troubling turn. She spent hours printing out Bible verses on index cards in a neat, almost hieroglyphic hand, and pasting them up above her bed. The verses were all of the same kind, and she arranged them in a particular order, one card above the other, like building blocks or a ladder:

'A man to whom God has given riches, but a stranger eateth it: this is vanity, and it is an evil disease.' Ecclesiastes 6: 2.

'By the great force of my disease is my garment changed: it bindeth me about as the collar of my coat.' Job 30:18.

'And healing all manner of sickness and all manner of disease among the people.' Matthew 4: 23.

'I will put none of these diseases upon thee, which I have brought upon the Egyptians.' Exodus 15:26.

It seemed she didn't read anything else, just these verses about healing and disease. With a precision unusual in one so young, she excised particular parts of whole verses, pasting up only the sections that would create this singular narrative of brokenness and reprieve, couched in images of bodies split between two poles. Seraphine knew of no-one except guzzum-wukkers who pasted up Scripture like that, over every available surface.

And in between, the child gathering paper-bags full of herbs, sorting, sorting, sorting under the house, using the chemistry kit, and scribbling in a binder notebook.

And ever her body bending lower and lower, like a woman seven times her age, her face growing more and more scrunched over her experiments, her eyes the only blaze in a face that seemed to have sucked up all her body's energy and pooled it incandescent into the sockets of the eyes. But at Granma Miss Crish's, when Seraphine went to visit her, Evangeline glowed like a shooting star.

The psychiatrist to whom Seraphine was referred pronounced Evangeline a normal, well-adjusted and particularly bright child. 'She does have a tendency to idealism, yes, but that is not a bad thing in one so young; quite the opposite, in fact. Believe me, we need a generation with dreams, mother. I wouldn't worry too much about the hobby – after all, Einstein is said to have been obsessed with playing cards as a child, and he didn't turn out too badly.' He smiled to reassure her.

'But why she looking like that? Don't you see she looks like an old woman, not a child? As if something else living inside her, feeding on her?'

The doctor looked startled. 'She looks perfectly normal to me,' he said abruptly, and Seraphine saw from his look that he was now thinking she was the one in need of psychiatric help.

It seemed that no-one but herself was able to see the wizened old woman standing in front of them in the clothes of the prepubescent girl.

The Adventist pastor, at the church where Seraphine was now fully restored, was equally unhelpful. 'I wouldn't be surprised if this young lady went into the medical profession,' he told Seraphine in front of her daughter after his private interview with the girl. 'The good book says the Lord gives us the desires of our hearts, and, you know, Mrs Morris, the desires of our hearts are easy to know, because they are the desires we had as a child, before we lost our innocence.'

The Baptist pastor, not the one who had officiated at the christening, was equally charmed by Evangeline; he too could see nothing wrong.

Seraphine wrestled with her religious convictions for an entire school year, but at last, begging God pardon for consulting with necromancers and unclean spirits concerning the very child over whose fate she had bargained with Him – begging pardon in advance and explaining herself in this way,

'Maasa God, people say all sort of thing and church have all sort of rule, but I see in your word where prophets came out of many places, not just Israel; did not Balaam the son of Beor also get message from you, down to him jackass?' – under cover of dawn she took Evangeline to a guzzum-lady three parishes away in St Helena.

The guzzum-lady trumped a deck of cards three times, and each time she shook her head and beetled her brow. Seraphine couldn't tell whether she looked frightened or angry. After the third throw she said, 'I cannot read this child, Mama. You are not honest. You are two-mouthed. Please leave. Leave.' And the guzzum-woman began to tremble with deep emotion, so that the ground shook under her feet.

Ashamed, Seraphine fled. Her daughter, who had been singularly silent on each of these forced pilgrimages, now stopped speaking to her altogether, and would no longer come home in the school holidays.

Seraphine was ready for war with teenager, but John counselled restraint. 'Seph,' he said, 'I know is your daughter and you love her. But you can't force her. You will only make things worse. Is not you alone – is a problem between mothers and their daughters, especially when they reach this age. Leave it, tek mi foolish advice an leave it. Give her time. It wi' work out.'

He did not mention the fact that Seraphine had always been suspicious of his mother, or that she had always felt she had married beneath her station. Indeed, John knew what no one else knew, that the source of Seraphine's heart-trouble over Evangeline was her distrust of his mother, rooted in a long-held and totally unfounded belief that the old woman worked obeah and had in fact obeahed John's father into the sexual relations that produced John and his younger brother. He was equally well aware of Seraphine's horrific self-conflict in having gone to the guzzum-woman, the way she had sought to rationalize this visit by telling herself that the guzzum-woman used her knowledge for good and not for evil. The woman was known to throw out of her yard anyone who came to ask her for spells to harm others, and so (Seraphine hoped) she must be a woman if not sent from God, at least not against Him either.

Festering in terror that it was only a matter of time before God blasted her for consulting with devils, and maybe setting more Satan on her child than had seemed to plague her before, Seraphine took her husband's advice. She tried to replace terror with praying, but she was haunted by the fear that God was too vex to hear her, particularly as she was not sure she was repentant.

Evangeline remained extremely polite, and extremely distant.

John, a man who accepted people, his wife, his children, and asked very few questions, remained close to his daughter, whom he visited when he could at his mother's house, bringing her ribbons, bright ornaments, pretty underwear, the foolish things men bring their daughters. Granma Miss Crish, like her beleaguered granddaughter, remained closed mouthed, but her buttoned-down lips spoke volumes.

No-one was able to say why, on Evangeline's sixteenth birthday, Seraphine changed her mind about letting the girl know of her dual citizenship. It may have been because Rita, returned from the USA after the latest of the yearly six-month stints by which she protected her permanent residency, had started prowling around again as if seeking either reconciliation or a new occasion for conflict. Perhaps Seraphine feared that Rita would take it upon herself to go down to Tekmihoe and tell the girl what was none of her, Rita's, business, in keeping with some ridiculous idea of coming-of-age entitlement that she had picked up in America.

Or perhaps Seraphine hoped for exactly the effect this information had on Evangeline, an effect that she hoped would part the child from her grandmother and the latter's unhealthy influence forever.

★

Evangeline finished her CAPE exams with straight A's and applied to university in England, to study not medicine, but anthropology and museum science. She won a scholarship to the University of Exeter.

On a fine day in September 2011, she boarded another British Airways flight to Gatwick Airport. It was her first journey away from Jacaranda, but as you are already aware, not her first journey away from or in search of home. And again, like an omen, in her handbag she had a sheaf of cards and on her iPod a flood of emails, both cards and emails saying, 'Happy birthday, Vangie, Evangeline.' It was the day she became seventeen years old.

And this was the contradiction of Evangeline, that she took all her journeys as if in obedience to some unheard voice, without a sound, without a murmur.

★

Two years of silence pass. Evangeline answers her telephone, perhaps, when her mother calls, and speaks in monosyllables, exceedingly polite. She laughs with her father, and on Father's day, his birthday, and Christmas, sends him brightly patterned cards with messages that his other eldest daughter, Beatrice, reads for him under the Home Sweet Home lamp that he still prefers to electricity, though even the outside kitchen is well wired.

Seraphine thinks of the shame this girl caused her, borning herself on an airplane in full view of strangers, and now this. And she weeps.

★

The year is 2012. Like a bombshell, out of the blue, Seraphine is now receiving letters from her daughter. She does not know whether the letters are to heal or provoke her.

September 14, 2012
I've been saved, sanctified, water-baptised, Holy Ghost filled, Jesus on my mind, I've found a new life, and I don't vex with you any more, Mummy.

Seraphine to herself: So does that mean she stop following guzzum ways and is behaving now like normal person?

October 21, 2012
This is a funny place, you know, Mummy. It is hard to

113

think of it as home, hard to believe that I'm really a citizen here. A man I met in Cambridge, I asked him the way to St Mary's Church because I wanted to see if it was really 300 steps to the front door, and why anyone would want to make it so hard for people to go into a church. The old, the lame, the halt or the blind couldn't go in there. Come to think of it, not the tired either, like how Jesus must have used to be tired. He asked me where I came from and I opened my mouth to say, 'I am English', but found I couldn't say it. So I told him I was from Jacaranda. And do you know what his answer was? 'Jacaranda, Jacaranda. That's where the rum and bananas come from, isn't it? Ah, the good old days of the British Empire.' And Mummy, do you know, he couldn't tell why I laughed and laughed and laughed until I couldn't stop. Finally, when he was looking really offended I said, 'I'm sorry, actually I'm English, I was just pulling your leg.' I doubt if he noticed that I said 'I'm from Jacaranda' in my English accent, but he did notice that I said, 'I'm English' in my Jacarandan accent. He was offended by that. 'You can't be, little miss,' he said. 'I'd know that accent anywhere.' I said, 'Have you been to Jacaranda?' He said no, but he'd know that accent any-where.

It sounds so crude, doesn't it? An encounter like that nearly 60 years after Independence. When we studied all of that in history class the British Empire seemed so long ago, another life. Something that happened to people long enough ago to be called ancestors, not to me.

Do you see why it's hard, Mummy? Yet I'm determined to claim my birthright. I'm not giving it away.

p.s. I often wonder why you gave me that birth certifi-cate.

Seraphine cussing raw. I didn't give it to you. Don't accuse me. You were born into it.

November 28, 2012
Thank you for my birth certificate, Mummy. You could

*have kept it from me, but you didn't. And I don't think it
was because you wanted to get rid of me. Today the sun
came out. Most times it is so cold here that I have started to
grow scales, like a fish. But in the market I can get any kind
of Jacarandan food I want. Callaloo, coconut, yam, dasheen,
all fresh snapper, grouper and my favourite, parrot fish,
straight off the boat. And plenty herbs – cinnamon leaf,
fever grass, sarsiperilla, red lovindeer bark. Still I have to
eat the fruits and vegetables here. I'm sure they're not half
as polluted as in the States, but still not as good as yours and
Gramps' ground provisions with the natural manure. So I
take no chances. Yesterday I started a washout with senna-
pod.*

Epsom salt is quicker. Or Phillips milk of magnesia. But no
doubt you think the bush-bush better. Though I have to admit
senna not bad. So which church yu going to, now that yu saved
and sanctified? Assembly of Jump-up?

*Yesterday in the market, I met a woman from Montserrat.
Her whole family was displaced by the volcano. She was
selling fabric and nutmeg in the market. She has never gone
back. A man was selling sea-cat at the meat stall; you know
I cannot stand the sight of sea-cat, I turned away in disgust.
He said hold on, I have something to show you. I didn't
want to 'hold on' but I was curious. He went and fetched,
you'd never guess what, Mummy. About a dozen cow cods,
each the length of two of my arms. I was so revolted I ran
out of there screaming.*

*It was a butcher from Newcastle. Funny, I always
thought we got the practice of eating them, or men eating
them, from the days of slavery when our people used to have
to eat the leftovers, so we learnt not to throw away anything.
Didn't know it was an English practice. Next week when
I go back I will ask him if here, as well, girls and women
aren't allowed to eat it for fear they get too sexy. At home you
adults always told us it was because we'd grow bald, but we
learnt the truth later – that it's an aphrodisiac.*

115

So are you learning anything useful in school, or is it all about wash-out and market and old wives' tales – yu learn anything yet yu granny don't teach yu? Apart from rudeness to yu mother?

Oh, I forgot to answer your question last time, Mummy. About church. I move around a bit. Checking them out. Two Sundays in a row the church near the campus didn't have a worship service. They were having a picnic instead. It's different from Jacaranda you know, Mummy. They don't take God so seriously.

Jesus keep me near the cross. What has become of this child?

Sometimes the letters were so totally perverse that Seraphine went on her knees in prayer and fasting. Evangeline took delight in relaying weird encounters that had a supernatural edge. For example, a year after she started writing to her mother, she began a serial story about a man she encountered at a bus stop in Exeter, and whom she kept having glimpses of in unexpected places, across crowded streets, at other bus stops, moving in and out of traffic, preaching.

The first time I saw him, Mummy, I thought I was right back there in Cedar Valley for the man was the living image of one of those mountain ecstatics, I mean madmen, that come down off the mountain robed and burning, shouting judgement like John the Baptist come again. In the middle of the summer he was dressed in a long coat and furry ankle boots with a knapsack on his back. (Though truth to tell it's so rarely we get real summer here, that maybe he was just making sure to 'be prepared', like a good boy scout, don't laugh, in case the sun went in and it started to sleet). He looked like a wild woodcutter except for the six-foot rod he was carrying, one long look-like-mahogany shaft carved in a fist at both ends, polished brown but the fist parts black. So strange to see someone like that in a place like this. In Birmingham they have a saying that England is a place make black people mad, but mostly it seems to be a genteel madness, very Victorian, not so – you know, nuff, not so nuff like this man. Funny though, maybe because I pray for him so much, I find myself starting to measure my life against the changes I see in him each time I glimpse him. I have a fancy we are parallel lines, running straight beside each other but never a chance of meeting, he in one direction, I completely opposite in the other. One of our faces turned backward.

Evangeline finished her degree in anthropology and displayed no interest in coming home. She stayed in school another two years, doing a masters in theology, then registered for a degree in medical law. Over the years the tenor of her letters changed, became urgent, and focused on family members instead of her experiences in England.

The first of this new series of letters, which began in 2014, was a shocking three sentence missive:

Mummy, who pregnant? Somebody in the family pregnant who not supposed to be. Is who?'

Two weeks later Aunt Mouse discovered sixteen-year-old Kyla vomiting her intestines out in the toilet. That was how the first of Evangeline's prophecies heralded the conception of my second cousin, Benjamin, and Aunt Mouse's war with the clan of Parkinson, to which the hapless father belonged. Aunt Mouse had to beat his name out of her daughter, but Joseph, barely sixteen-years-old himself, had already anticipated this showdown and just at the moment when Kyla, on her knees and sobbing, 'Do Mama, do, is Joseph but a nuh fi him fault alone,' had given up in despair, he walked into our yard and owned up to his responsibility. How Evangeline, all the way in Exeter, UK, knew that it took three strong men – Uncle Titty, Davidow and my father – to get Aunt Mouse off the boy is one of the mysteries of who Evangeline came to be. No-one told her anything, not even that someone was really pregnant, but she phoned my mother to tell her to tell Aunt

Mouse to stop behaving like an irrational woman and forgive and support her daughter as Jesus commanded.

From then on, Evangeline seemed to have set herself up as a watchdog over the fates and fortunes of our vast family. She foresaw with frightening accuracy every danger that would beset us, every folly or risk we would commit. Apart from that first raw question that hit on Kyla's pregnancy, her predictions never arrived by themselves but surrounded by dark prophecies and kabbalistic sayings, like a single white egg crouched in a wide, covered basket. Into this basket, which I always imagined as a fishpot made of dark green reeds, my sister plaited doctrines, rebukes, corrections, instructions, warnings, exhortations, calls to repentance, encouragements, urgings, preachings, foreshadowings, dreams, Bible verses, visions, unwelcome advice, abrasively righteous opinions, all manner of practical and spiritual paraphernalia that fascinated, terrified and alienated us so that we lived in constant shame of the things she would discover about us. And yet some of us, I certainly, petrified as I was, could not help deriving a sense of special protection from the fact of having a seer in the family. It was from that time that we dropped the diminutive Sister Vangie, and started speaking of her as Evangeline the Prophet, Four-Eye Evangeline and, behind our mother's back, Evangeline the obeah-woman. From across the distance of two oceans she became our moral compass, so irresistible a conscience, although she never came home, that by tacit consent we kept everything in the family that she did not predict, secret from her. In my heart I sometimes laughed at ourselves, because the image of us that came to my mind was of little children discovered playing hide-and-seek behind mesh-wire fences, fiercely holding their place behind the mesh and protesting that they were not giving up because they had not yet been found. When she wrote complaining that we never told her anything, that we treated her like a stranger, not a member of the family, we received this as the intrusion of an outsider with no class who had already, without permission, seen and judged too much of our nakedness and didn't have the basic upbringing to know she was out of order. Holding fiercely to our right to sin, and privacy in which to do it, we felt both guilt and gladness that Evangeline felt left out, as if we had been victors in an unsanctioned, internecine war.

Not everyone felt this way about Evangeline. In fact, without having seen any of us in seven years, and without having lived with us for much longer, she divided the family into camps as surely as a surgeon's knife divides tissue: those who became fiercely loyal to her (a minimal camp of probably one, Tramadol, and Tram's echo-in-waiting, Pete, who we regularly suspected of feeding to Evangeline the inside information that returned to us as prophecy); those, the cowardly, who played the role of independents and suspended judgment on Evangeline on the basis of 'different strokes for different folks'; and the majority party, those of us who remained befuddled, torn, resentful, and in love with her.

It didn't help that Evangeline was not only after our souls but also our material well-being. Our parents were not destitute, but times were hard and the family was large, the yearly births seemingly endless. Evangeline always held some kind of job while pursuing her studies, and she took it upon herself to assist with the schooling of particular siblings and cousins. She decided who and when based on some form of lottery known only to herself, although according to Tramadol, who in her own way was just as mystic, Evangeline's system was really quite methodical and egalitarian, ensuring an equal spread between boys and girls, targeting the families with the greatest need, dropping one and taking up another when she felt the child had reached a stage sufficient to manage with less, or on its own, or was able to get a job. It was easy to be grateful for her care and damn vexed at the interference she seemed to think this purchased for her.

Tramadol, the characteristically silent, voiced a different opinion, and of course Pete, who had no mind of his own when Tram was around, echoed her viewpoint. 'She dream about us because of blood,' Tram said, in that cryptic way of speaking that she had caught like a disease from listening to Evangeline's once-a-month letters that our mother read to us around the dinner table.

'How yu mean, because of blood?' B asked aggressively, puffing her large chest out like hen's feathers.

'Is how the vein that hold us to her press on her brain,' Tram elaborated. 'It carry message like wireless, like internet. Das how she dream wi pain.'

'Huh,' B scoffed. 'She too love preach, is what. This Jesus business mek har mad.'

'Holy Spirit,' Truck interjected, grimacing.

'What yu mean, Holy Spirit?'

'She say is Holy Spirit reveal all dem tings to her. Foolishniss.'

The familiar uneasy silence descended. None of us liked the thought that maybe we were blaspheming; at the same time, none of us wanted to think that unless we went Evangeline's way we would not reach heaven's gate and see Jesus.

A few months before she came back home, Evangeline returned to stories of herself, among them stories of her encounters with the mountain man of Exeter, whom we had all but forgotten. Either the mountain man was still on the streets after three and a half years, or Evangeline derived pleasure from relaying, in retrospect, events that had taken place long before.

She discovered that the mountain man was not from Jacaranda or anywhere in the Caribbean but from an African country. One day she went up near enough to him to hear what he was preaching at the sky, his small mouth moving, she said, like a disturbed worm or a rolling plum lost in the bushy knolls of his beard. She could not contain any longer her curiosity at the way he preached, not down at or across the crowds, but looking skyward and shaking his staff at an unseen assailant up there, who filled him with rage. 'I couldn't understand a word of what he was saying,' Evangeline wrote. 'Only the accent. I think it was Nigerian. And he wasn't preaching at us, he was preaching at God.' We laughed at the picture of the man exhorting God to behave himself.

Once a year she saw him, and each time he seemed to have deteriorated further. At some point he lost or gave up his rod and appeared at the bus stop almost hidden from sight behind a massive billboard hung around his neck, decorated with all manner of Scripture promising brimstone, fire, apocalypse and bakery in hell's kitchens for the unrepentant. When she crossed the street to read his billboard, he had already started to move off, but he saw her coming and waited for her with the graciousness of a host holding open a door for his guest. But the way he stood, full frontal, waiting until she had read it all, reminded her of nothing so much as of a mother breastfeeding a nervous, half-drowsy child, holding herself very still in case the child sensed an impulse of withdrawal and waked crying. This image of ghastly intimacy, of a wild man feeding Evangeline milk from his breasts, made my mother more irritated than usual with her daughter's antic descriptions, and she kissed her teeth and threw the letter down. Evangeline made the rest of us laugh. It was odd how, despite her petrifying seriousness, her letters often sent us into stitches.

The following year she said the man was preaching with a fly whisk, neither rod nor billboard anywhere in sight. In all the years, he hadn't changed his clothes.

In the summer of 2024, the family received a last letter from Evangeline.

Yesterday in the pharmacy a woman followed me around from aisle to aisle, shelf to shelf, like she was my shadow. When I turned around to rebuke her, ask her if is because I black she think I tief something that she lost, she gave me an embarrassed smile, asked me if I had yet made my will, and handed me a card from the law firm where she worked. I nearly drop down. I so taken aback I look in the mirror by the reading glasses rack where we were standing, to see if my hair had suddenly gone gray or my back bend in two, though I still seeing myself same height from the ground. I look at her and I answer, 'Time to go home. I don't know where, but I going.'

In the same letter she reported her last sighting of the mountain man. She ran into him in a Fedex copy centre, scanning pages from a leaflet that was not his, something he might have picked up off the street, because clearly he was no longer mentally well.

All the members of the immediate family that were still living at home, and as many cousins as it could hold, crammed into a hired van to meet Evangeline at the airport.

I had not seen my sister in thirteen years.

One or two idlers from the district attached themselves to various perilous parts of the van – the step, the open boot – and came along with us, tickled by the outing and the thought of early ingratiating themselves into Evangeline's foreign pocket-book. My mother, who had no intention of allowing Evangeline to be coerced into giving any handouts, nevertheless suffered them, not knowing how, once again in front of people, she would be shamed.

The hangers-on were not the only ones. It seemed that the whole district was at the airport to behold my mother's shame. It was two weeks before Christmas, and the place was so crowded with the relatives of foreign Jacarandans escaping from the northern cold that there was no room for most of us at the barrier ropes that cordoned off the waiting area. The family had to stand in a vertical line with strong B at the head hanging on to her part of the rope, thrusting her Mount Everbreast bosom forward so that no-one could push her to where she would be lost in the crowd and not see Evangeline when she emerged.

Evangeline came through the terminal doors looking like nobody we knew. There was no family resemblance at all. Nevertheless my mother recognized her at once, and let out a terrible, inadvertent wail, like a woman who has anticipated bad news in a dream and seen it confirmed.

'Rahtid, shi a Nyahbingi,' Derek, one of the idlers, whispered in awe.

'No, a nuh Rasta dat, dat a Converter. Rasta wear red, green and gold.'

It was neither. The truth was, Evangeline was dressed in the most outlandish costume any of us had ever seen on someone who was supposed to be educated. We had known England was a place that sent black people mad, but not that mad. She was wearing a bright-bleached calico gown, a loose shift really, wrapped at the waist with a girdle of blue, purple and red, and on her head something like a Pope's mitre, made either of gold papier mache or some satiny, papery cloth, with the words 'Holiness unto the Lord' picked out in red embroidery and underlined by tassels that hung beneath them, just above her eyebrows. A vast array of tassels and pins hung from a lapel that ran right across the front of the shift, above her breasts. Her wrists too were accoutred with tassels like multicoloured bracelets, above a pair of fingerless gloves. Later, as we sat beside each other in the van, I counted the memorials engraved in photographs on the pins or embroidered in legends on the tassels: Marcus Garvey and Amy-Jacques; Winnie and Nelson Mandela; Martin Luther and Coretta Scott King; Mother Theresa; William Knibb; William Wilberforce; Alexander Bedward; Rex Nettleford; Fidel and Dalia Castro; Nanny of the Maroons; Pandora; Scheherazade. She also had little, intricately engraved packets, the shape and half the size of matchboxes, hanging from an embroidered overpiece at her neckline. In it, we were to discover, was a tiny computer disk with photographs of the entire Pointy-Morris clans. Around her neck she wore a plain wooden cross that rested in the middle between the tassels and pins on right and left.

The truth was I had never seen anyone look so royally attired, so wondrously garnished in the glory of the hues of creation. The colours shimmered and glowed, with a glowing that seemed to be made of original dyes, in the heart of the earth where colour was first born. The purples shifted to blue black and then to midnight mauve with a touch of lavender that caressed the rippling shades of blue (aqua, lapis and sweet indigo), the reds more crimson than poppies, and wet with their richness, even as the gold cloth was wet to vermillion in its folds and the texture of corn and wheat fields where it was smooth. Colour rumoured with colour, clamoured, merged, receded, ran in quiet rills, melted into one glorious abstract in which only the pure white of her gown stood out as background and, under the hot Jacaranda sun, the jewel

colours of trees, cultivated airport flowers and sky kow-
towed and dimmed. She looked like an art exhibition by a
master painter awoken at midnight with the rage of his
calling upon him.

Two red-cap porters were pushing enormous mounds of
baggage on either side of Evangeline. 'God Almighty, a how
one smaddy can have so much bag? A soldier camp she a go
feed?' Derek, the chatterbox one-third of the idlers, was
breathing reverently behind me.

Later, when we opened the bags, I thought she had brought
all of England in her suitcases for us and for the district, like
someone haunted by the milk of human kindness, or, as
Tramadol said, by the hurt of belonging.

When my mother cried that night, everyone had gone to
bed exhausted, and I was the only one who heard – though I
wondered whether those two haunted ones, Tramadol and
Pete, were awake and heard her too.

'Can you imagine,' my mother travailed with her God, 'I
make so much sacrifice to give her a good education, I sacrifice
my feelings to send her away from foolishness, to give her her
birthright, and this is what she turn out to be. Not right in her
head. All those degrees, and she not right in her head.'

My mother is a woman who has produced a child for each
of the elements. Beatrice, feet firmly planted, is my mother's
earth child. I, Micheline, they say, belong to the waves of the
sea, constantly changing, unable to tell a straight truth. My
mother hates that about me. She worries about Pete, who, she
says, looks like quicksilver, but in reality is too light, easily
catching fire, a child of October, when the leaves in America
fall.

The air in the stratosphere at 35,000 feet, pressure at 250
millibars, 25 kpa, 3.6 psi, can play havoc with a child's inner
formation. Here collects most of the water that exists in the
atmosphere. Most of the clouds that occupy our weather
systems. Most of the matter and chemicals carried by fires,
volcanoes, hurricanes, floods, power plants, nuclear fissions,
heaters, air conditioners, portable tv sets, refrigerators, washing machines, microwaves, cars, buses, trucks, trains, trac-

tors, bobcats, cranes, plastic water bottles, scandal bags, exhumed bodies, concertinas, and lungs screaming in madness, agony, love, or rage. Most of the earth's long love and suffering with humans. Travelling upwards, near to the bare feet of God.

There is little enough left to tell. The rest you will discern from the ghost of my sister's presence haunting all the other confessions in this book.

Whether Seraphine was within her rights or not to feel her labour had been wasted never hindered Evangeline. Since the year of her return, she has been preaching in the streets, warning on the roads, keeping vigil at the crossroads, rebuking in the churches, exhorting our children, feeding and lambasting the idlers, washing the indigent, nursing the sick, volunteering in the jails, volunteering in the schools (where she teaches the children history using the legends and photographs inscribed on her pins, tassels and phylacteries), attending global conferences on medical anthropology (her last hop was in Rome), giving lectures at universities where the auditoriums are bound to be full because nobody knows when Evangeline will break out into searing prophecy in the midst of giving an erudite paper on the poetics of plant life among the indigenous peoples of the Amazon. At the back of her house in the hills of Bypass, next door to Aunt Rita, she keeps a little herbarium, where she nurtures, plucks and sorts bush-bush, boils and mixes them in pipettes, and scribbles shorthand in a bound notebook. From some of these bushes, and from packets sent in careful wrappings from England, she makes her own dyes, which she uses to stain rolls of plain calico that she gives away free. When Granny Miss Crish died at the age of a hundred and one, it was Evangeline who performed the last rites and closed her eyes.

To this day, none of us knows what the bargain was that Seraphine made with God. But over the years my mother has grown reconciled because of all the people who, by their own testimony, mad Evangeline has helped.

FRAGMENT

I am the one who wasn't expected to write anything because I am not a book person. Plus Mitch is not the kind of person who you can trust not to go in there and interfere with what don't concern her, fixing full stop and comma and all that kind of nonsense, and I don't like people trouble my things when I put them down. I don't like the one Evangeline either for she too holy-holy, and too love treat the rest of us like we is her children, and it really upsetting to see how she get Mitch to write her part of the story so she would get the most space, for she well and know Mitch cannot stop once she start, she going write until the page feel pain and cry out for murder. Chuups. Like she tink word can tun flesh and mek gunman or duppy flee. She think any story pon earth can finish? But you know, Pete was my brother too and this supposed to be a family album for him so I might as well put in my two cents.

Mitch don't say anything about me so let me introduce myself. I am Peaches, number five in the family, unless you count Tram, who I think of as more like Pete twin, though she not our sister but really our cousin. In which case I am still not number six, if you count Pete and Tram as half each. Think of me as the fifth figure in this quadrille Mitch and them dancing. I come in pon the side, unexpected. Pass di kutchie pon di lef' han side. Nuh so? But I going keep it short, so Mitch can squeeze me in without cutting and carving and telling more lie so I can fit.

So as I was saying, I am Peaches. Otherwise called Cynthia, my right name. The rough and tough one who dress in big boots and work on construction site like man. I never run after school like the rest. In that way I suppose you could say I am just like Tram, big laugh, woiie yoii! I do a Associate in

Construction and that was enough for me. I like being outside making things, sensible things like house that people can live in, not pretty pretty things for people to just look on or read. I have seven children, one less than my mother, and I bring them up under one roof but not with their father. He live by himself and I live by myself, for to bring man in your house is pure sin, shame and disgrace. But I have no quarrel with him otherwise; he is a good father to his children.

Yes, Peaches. The one who like to go to court to watch proceedings, even when they don't concern me. My sisters and brothers laugh and find it funny, say I have nuff blue boot fi climb eleven step, but is a lot of things I learn from watching proceedings in court. The strangest things happen there. What people bring and how people lie is unbelievable. Up to recently I see a rape case throw out of court because the supposed victim married to the raper the very next day after the rape suppose fi tek place. And a man bring up a man fi tiefing him banana five days after him warn him him was going to tief it. Say the man shoulda tief it same day as the warning, so the man wouldn't have ketch him unawares. I see how those people bold and brave to bring foolishness to judge and so I was never afraid to talk out in court. I learn from every idiot.

I feel bad over how Pete die, yes, but I don't feel guilty like the rest of them saying. I do what I have to do for Pete. I was the one stand up in court and tell the judge the truth, that Avette deliberately make herself a unreliable witness by changing her story over and over so they wouldn't call her to give evidence. I stand up and tell the court that Maryam lying through her mash-up mash-up teeth, I tell them the police take bribe to hide the murder weapon that all of a sudden-so nobody cannot find. I tell you the rahtid truth, if I did have the money, I sue every last blasted one of them in civil court, the government, the police, Avette, Maryam. This wicked country where murderation is dime a dozen because nobody in charge don't care, for they get paid to damn corrupt. I never agree with Evangeline or the lawyers who advise us to let it go because of shortage of evidence and how we couldn't force

Avette to testify. Me, I woulda force her, she wouldn't know what hit her. I don't shame or feel guilty, is only because I didn't have the money. They should have a system where you can appeal against an acquittal, same as how you can appeal against a conviction.

The other thing is how everybody going on like Pete was a saint, that's why I don't like eulogy, you know, I don't want any of that at my funeral, you hear. Pete wasn't no saint, him was flesh and blood same way and have some dutty ways just like the rest of us, and the only dream I dream see him after him dead is when I see him dress up neat in him burying clothes, working behind a fence, looking sober and serious, like a man who sit down and think about what him doing with himself for the first time. I say to him 'Hi Pete,' and he greet me back, and I say, 'How things over there?' and he say, 'Things not bad, but you know, if I did tek advice, I would be over there where you are now.'

What you say? No, nutten nuh do mi. Is just that I feel like cussing a whole set of badwud because I can't stop this eyewater from making me fall down.

IV

SONG

To live is to fly!
So shake the dust off of your wings
And the sleep out of your eyes!
        — Townes van Zandt

Seh. Seh knowing how to live
Is just learning how to die!
Seh Jah-Jah give you wings
Man, cleave the sky!
        — Davidow Pointy Morris (Jah Crown)

And now, the house in the forest is bejewelled. No one can say how it was that the snails which fell on their backs became moonstone, or the ones crawling straight became sardonyx. It is difficult to see the house through the trees now grown ruinate, but the encrustations shine in the green darkness, beckoning. The ropes of wiss-wiss, massed heliconia, bush-bush and macka where the tended garden had been, before the big rains, have grown up so thick they look like they could not be breached in a hundred years. But searchers have found a path through the overgrowth, bending low, almost on hands and knees, to come through to the clearing.

Not many come here any more. Most of the district and townspeople have moved away to the hills, to escape the encroaching sea, which is being driven steadily inland by the earth's fevered convulsions. Moreover, they became afraid of the dwarf-child.

'Witch-baby!'

'Heaven help, what is that half-child prophesying? It curdle mi bone!'

'Curdle mi sleep! Is like a angel passing.'

The open doorway of the house faces the clearing, in the middle of which is set, in an old sugar-plantation copper, a small round lake, salt and daily shrinking, evaporated by the sun's unnatural heat. Yet inside here, at 100 degrees Fahrenheit in the shade, it is several degrees cooler than outside. The heat is softened by the massed undergrowth and the sweeping branches of the mahogany and cedar trees, which have changed their shape in search of water, leaning down to touch the grass, as in the old days willows and mangroves used to do. Now most of those have died. The clearing seems magical, enchanted, the grass fiery green under a strangely lambent looking sun, the dragonflies, wildflowers and, once, a hummingbird, sparking the undergrowth like the flash of jewels.

It is because of the dwarf-child's song. The grey woman is amazed again at the miracle, that flowers grow here so lushly and the few remaining insects still come to sip the nectar; amazed that the speechless child draws them, when he is happy, with the sweet unearthly keening that issues from his formless lips, behind the white membrane. The sound of it is purer than spun glass, or bells at matins when the sky used to be coloured rose, or gold, or blue. Today, even the sky seems clearer than it has for years, as if some inhabitant of the planets has taken a trowel and rolled back the layer of dark brown mud. But the village is afraid of the dwarf-child's song.

Micheline sets the computer screen to triple x definition and scrolls up the book, watching the print, images and graphics settle into their assigned places. The house, the clearing, the forest, the grey woman with the dwarf-child, her and her sister's faces, come into view. She clicks on the mousetab, watches everything make somersaults, arrange itself into random stories, new pictures. Finally their two faces swim into focus once more, as if tired of the game, and she says to herself, It is time. In truth, the game has been a delaying tactic, a sleight of hand in which her mind has not been at all involved. She feels that where this collection of pages is concerned she has no real control. Playing Scheherazade is with her more than an obsession – it is an addiction. Nothing pumps the excited blood in her veins more than the changing stories, the multiple finishes, or no finishes, that the web has made possible. But to confront again the book of reversals, in which she herself is changing, like water changes around boulders, is a different matter altogether. Unnerving. Still, reneging is not an option. She has involved the others, her siblings, in this project. She must see it through to the end. She lets the pages settle into their original frame, back to the shape in which the scene and their spoken words had uploaded when she and her sister sat talking through the long night to daybreak.

The grey woman is mending a wound in the dwarf-child's foot. It is not a new wound; it has opened time and time again, before. The flesh, leering beneath the torn suture, has the look of uncooked mince. She sews it up expertly and swiftly, as the medics have shown her, using the special thread from the space hospital. The wound hurts a little, but the dwarf-child is happy, full of questions. He is not yet able to speak, but he has learnt to write his questions on the tele-slate on his arm, attached to the white membrane which serves him for skin, and the speed of the writing, question tumbling upon question, and the low hum of his keening, tells the woman he is happy. When he is not, the sound is like a wild beast's howl, raw and feral, and red spots sprinkle the membrane in which he is encased.

'When they come for me on Monday, will they come in a cyberchute or will they pull me through the Intertube, I'd like that, to ride in a tunnel under the sea, whooey. When they're done, will I have skin like yours, Momma will the doctor cut my throat, just to see if they can make me talk, just in case? But suppose they cut it wrong, I don't think I'd like that. No, better not, better leave that out. Until they run further tests. For now they can just do my hair and skin. I will have hair won't I, Momma?'

The grey woman tries to answer as best she can, finding words to shield his happiness and allay his fears, which are not all that different from her own.

This Evangeline no longer wears her medals, pins or plaques, and her clothes are not carnival-royal as when she was young, but grey with a hint of lavender, like the heart of a sea-jewel. These days she teaches only the dwarf child, though in the beginning she had kept him with the others, thinking that he should have company, like a normal child, and they in their turn would learn acceptance, and the love of giving. But it soon became clear that the dwarf-child might not survive the extremes of cruelty and compassion of which children are capable, and so she closed the Wednesday evening and Saturday school on her front verandah, and sent the children home. She misses them, the sound of their feet drumming on the floor, the wide-open ackee-seed shine of their eyes full of questions, mischief, wonder, their exigent judgements that allowed adults no quarter, their heedless play, the sharp intensity of their loves and quarrels. And in truth, despite her fears she would have kept them on, risking the dwarf-child to time and grace, except that increasingly he needed full-time care, and moreover the families of these children needed to take to the hills with the rest of those who were too poor to run off the coasts of the islands, pushing boats out in search of undiscovered seas, where they hoped the ozone threat would not come, and some part of the overheated, agitated planet would be still. A vain hope, but the heart must go on living.

A few of the few remaining in the district still come to say howdy-do, and to hear her tell a story, once in a blue moon – but fewer and fewer, as the children die, or their parents move away. She had not seen a single one come through the hedge, in more than half a year.

But yesterday the undergrowth was busy. A straggle of little ones burst through, come to cadge goodies from her oven and with undiminished curiosity call on the dwarf child, almost as if they knew these were his last days in the jewelled house. The dwarf-child worked tirelessly all day, showing off his mansion which, with the school gone, was all his alone once more. And having been by himself so long, with obsequy instead of shame he seduced the visitors, letting the wondering tips of fingers touch his membrane while they asked him curious questions:

'How come you bigger now? How you grow without skin?'

'You can open your mouth now? Your mouth grow open

138

yet?' The ones who are old enough to read recite his answers eagerly from the tele-slate, the others wondering at the magic of his song.

'What colour you see me in? You can see colours in their right colour now?'

'Blue! You are a blue boy, woie!' The dwarf-child teases them, giggling. She sees that he is holding his own. Still, in between distracting them with baked things, the craved story and a puppet show, she hovers in the background of their play, ready to grab furtive hands pushing food or waste at his throat.

'Eat, dwarf-boy! Yu modda seh yu mus eat it!'

She saw and was upset that several of them were suffering from skin ailments, for which she gave them salve she had made from herbs. The girls were ashamed, but some of the boys showed off their patches, whose carbuncle was bigger, don't my skin redder than yours where it peel off? And 'Look, boy, I will burst boil in your face! I can make it fly further than you can pee!'

She was glad they came, because soon the dwarf-child would be going to a place where there were other children, who also would look at him with astonished eyes. It was good for him to get used to this curiosity again, ahead of time, even if only for the few hours that the district children stayed. The dwarf-child was happy, and sang all day, though he howled afterwards, angry that they came and left. This morning he refuses to remember their coming. He turns resolutely away from where the overgrowth is still agitated with the residue of childish energy, a vibration as if something more should happen.

Yet the dwarf-child seems by himself to be a million children in one. Especially the questions. From an early age, almost before he was out of diapers, he would tire her out with questions. Most often, questions about space. As if such questions were encrypted in his DNA. As if he knew, from the day he was conceived, that he would be called a sky child.

Before he was four, she bought him a space encyclopaedia, which he downloaded himself on his cyber-slate. The infra-red collar flashed and glinted, tracking the astounding brainwaves even as it allowed him to see. In no time at all he had the whole book by heart, and exhausted her with new, impossible questions. But he still likes to ask the old ones. Turning everything into a game, he invents new answers, bored by those he already knows by heart. What made the sky brown, when in the picture books it was blue? Did somebody imagine another kind of sky? What kept the space hospital in orbit, how were nano-engines made? What did the mind of a space computer look like, could you trace its thoughts by changes in its colour the way you could trace his changes by the blood that showed under the white membrane he had in place of skin? What lay beyond the universe, and God?

'God,' she tells him, smiling.

He nods vigorously in understanding, the VISOR-collar* holding the head safely on its too-delicate stalk. 'Huh-huh. More God. God and God and God and God and God. Lots of God. Gods!'

'No. One God, stretching on and on forever.'

'Like elastic! Whooeey! The longest elastic in the wooooooo – .' Giggling, he pulls away from her to write the series of 'o's on his body instead of the tele-slate, too impatient to wait for the scroll-down. He writes them in looped coils over his arm, continues down and across his chest, bending to continue down his thighs, legs, and feet, pretends to write behind his back as well. When he gets to his toes, he finishes the word triumphantly with a squinched-up 'orld!'

He scrolls away the beginning of the sentence to write on the slate, 'The world is bigger than God, look!'

'It's only that God is bigger than Himself, Smarty Pants. And bigger than your clever little head. Here, let me finish this.'

Shaking with laughter, pleased with himself for teasing her, he allows her to seal the bandage. His pleasure breaks out in a piercing, wordless song, as though he had turned a somersault and thrown a hat of song into the air.

---

* Visual Instrument and Sensory Organ Replacement (from *Star Trek: The Next Generation*).

The most astonishing thing of all is that the disease has left his mind unimpaired; indeed, by the bizarre turns with which these days are familiar, may even have been the cause of his strange genius. This causes her great pain, for it means he might not survive for long, but at the same time the greatest gladness and wonder, that so much of his child's beauty has survived intact.

The dwarf child thinks that perhaps he might fly.

'You'd like to be an astronaut.'

'No, not that,' he tells her scornfully. 'Be'ond the planets. Where everything ends.'

She corrects the spelling of 'beyond' for him. He ignores her.

'And then, what? When you get to where everything ends.'

He considers this, frowning. The frown registers as a dark ball of blood across his forehead. 'Changeover. Be like everybody else. Nose, mouth, skin. Talk. Better than they can make me in the hospital. Better!'

The grey woman's heart aches, smiles for the dwarf child, his dream of heaven a dream of belonging, right here on earth. And I John saw a new earth, the holy city, new Jerusalem, coming down from God out of heaven, prepared.

But the dwarf child is inventive, endlessly resourceful, and fickle, as children are. He has changed his mind and wants instead to sail on water. There, that is much better. Though for what reason this is better, he does not say. 'With wings,' he adds, nodding to himself with satisfaction.

'Hovercraft. You want to sail in a hovercraft,' she teases him, already expecting the objection from this child who so completely despises the narrowness of adult inventions. 'They travel at 1000 miles an hour.'

'No, silly!' The dwarf-child bobs his head at her, wondering why she is being so stupid, the way adults are stupid. Angrily he sketches a bird gliding on the sea, wings splayed out wide. 'Like that! Nobody makes them! They just are!'

'Of course,' she says, soothing. 'It would be great to be a seabird, and skate on the water.'

The dwarf-child looks scornful. He knows she is humouring him.

'Not a bird. Me.'

'Okay, boss man, I hear you. And off you go. Reading time.' She watches him smiling as he scrambles off to his box-seat under the playroom window. He will be happy for the next half hour reading his space stories, before she calls him, or he calls her, for his recess. He will sing under his breath as he reads, and the song will fill the room with odours.

The dwarf-child is not really a dwarf; he is the right size for a child of six, but people call him a dwarf because of the size of his head, which is too large for the delicate stalk of his neck and has to be held up by the infrared collar which also helps him to see. His eyes are gleaming and glowing but without the collar there are colours he cannot see. With it, he can see things no-one else can see. The dwarf-child is not an albino; nobody has been told what race he is. He is white all over because he was born without a skin, encased instead in a membrane the colour of watered milk, so white it glimmers blue at the edges, like glimpses of an opal. The membrane is wrapped around his flesh in the same way that skin is wrapped, as if someone had put him in it to protect his flesh and delicate organs while his skin, which had been forgotten, was being made. Under the membrane the shape of his features is clearly outlined, and most of them are perfectly formed, so that people seeing him think that probably he was meant to be a beautiful child. But his lips are somewhat blurred, as if whoever was carving them had not quite finished, and instead of ears he has earholes, set flat against his head. The earholes have been covered with a telephonic filter, so that he can endure the world of sound. Without the filter, the dwarf-child hears sound unbearably magnified, in thunders, high-pitched screams and Atlantic groanings. The filter keeps the dwarf-child's head from exploding.

All his capillaries, veins and arteries seem to be near the surface. They are visible under the flesh, which flushes with various shades of blood when the dwarf-child is excited, so that the white membrane appears at different times to be stained with a reflection of colours thrown by some hidden source of light. The membrane is not a skin. It is like a transparent casing under a skin, shaped and contoured around the live body which it hems in.

The dwarf-child's eyes are shining, dark and deep, like great wells, or distant space at night. When he was born, he could not move his toes or fingers; the membrane had grown over and encased them so that they were like clubs. But fingers and toes were visible under the casing and the doctors were able to help his hands and feet break free. The dwarf-child is able to manipulate objects that are not sharp, and to walk with the stumbling gait of a man on the moon, wearing soft gloves on his hands and suede coverings on his feet. In the past few months of treatment, his hands and feet have begun to grow a pinky-brown skin, which the doctors hope will harden to a proper human shell and, with more treatment, spread to cover the entire membrane. There are unseen parts of him missing. The doctors will finish shaping his lips, but have not yet worked out how to give him speech, beyond the wordless singing. They are not sure they can truly construct the organs of his throat – because of some unusual quirk in his make-up, stem-cell cultures have not taken. But they think they can, perhaps, fit him with an artificial voice-box that will not give him allergies. It is the allergies that have slowed down his treatment.

She calls the dwarf-child 'he', as everyone else has done, but it is not clear what sex the dwarf-child is, because his genitals are fused. She thinks to herself that she has accepted 'he', because one of her siblings, a brother, is missing. Her brother was murdered. She thinks that the dwarf-child has been sent to stand for her brother's continuing generations.

The dwarf-child calls her 'Momma'; he has been given relatives and a family tree, but he does not know who his parents really are.

No one has been told the dwarf-child's origins. An aban-doned child, he was found knotted into the foetal position, and was unbent with forceps. The stories of how he got here were as numerous as there were people to tell them. According to one version, the dwarf-child was a history-book written in flesh, a throwback to half a century ago, when wars were fought in a certain way. It was said that an Iraqi diplomat holidayed on Jacaranda's north coast with his wife, who fell in love with a Rastaman and defected to the foothills to live with him in sin, leaving her husband to return home alone. But the Iraqi woman's genes had been contaminated with American plutonium from the 9/11 war, and the children she had with the Rastaman, and their children after them, were born with this taint, which showed itself in deformities of body or mind, or both. The dwarf-child was either the Iraqi woman's grand or great-grand child.

This version was not as popular as the one in which the dwarf-child was a half-aborted foetus, left on the riverbank one before-day morning by the ghosts of slave women who had fished him from the river where his unknown mother, terrified by his deformities, had thrown him to drown.

Alternatively, he was one of a famous pair of twins born in the space hospital in orbit around the moon. The true story of these twins was well publicized, reaching quickly by webnews even to Jacaranda's remotest districts. Neither child had survived, but one had mysteriously disappeared. The missing child, it was said, had been dumped by space parachute over the fields of Jacaranda, because the doctors needed to cover-up his deformities – evidence that the space experiment was not working – but because of some strange twist of compassion, they had not had the heart to kill him outright. Maybe they hoped that in this far outpost some primitive form of wonder might save him. Apparently it had. The space twins had been born over twelve years ago, twice the time since the dwarf-baby was found, but the dwarf-child was too good an occasion for such a legend to miss.

No, some said, the dwarf-child was Evangeline Morris's secret love-child, which she could not own outright without disgracing her profession as a preacher. A love-child, the fruit of a swelling womb easily disguised under the wide robes of gold, scarlet, purple and finally grey that she wore. Or perhaps the dwarf-child was the fruit of incest, the union of two cousins who had breached the boundaries. The grey woman suspected that though some of these inventions were the product of malicious gossip, her sister Micheline was behind not a few of the more creative ones. A story-maker with an antic sense of humour, Micheline would not have allowed herself to resist telling curious inquisitors what they wanted to hear, each time she was accosted.

Micheline, word-weaver, who, the grey woman reflects smiling, could never tell a straight truth. This trait she has passed on to her nephew Davidow, Davidow her dead brother's son, a boy of fisticuffs turned restless singer, calling himself now Jah Crown, who would come in the morning to calibrate from the dwarf-child's humming a new song. His father had begged with his dying words that he would not fight, not beat up on people, and so Davvy now makes music with the hands that used to punch flesh.

Micheline. Could never tell a straight truth. And yet how even Micheline had longed, in the face of death, for a single steadfast truth, one burning spear of it, no more!

The thought of her sister turns the grey woman's eyes inward, to the memory of a long sadness. *The computer screen blinks, uploading the memory.* Micheline and she, Evangeline, clutching each other by the arms, forehead to forehead on their knees on a bare wooden floor, clutching, and breaking away with pain, Micheline's anguish a cow-bawling more raw than the dwarf-child's rage, hers a mewling like a sick child's. She unable to cry aloud, because of the knife in her side, under the rib. The knife under her rib is the memory-trace of the knife that killed her brother, a knife that lodged in her side for three successive nights before he was killed. From these dreaming prognostications to the sharp reality of time and breaking day, at sudden, unexpected moments, like an unannounced visitor at the door, comes this sensation of a keen cut through the heart that leaves her pinned in place wherever she is standing, or sitting, or lying, unable to move or die. She has longed for the comfort she has given to others, to Micheline now, Micheline hating herself, weeping as if her heart had not only broken but had long lost its gates, blaming herself, as we all have done, for loving our brother too little, for not doing enough, for making privacy, freedom, manhood an excuse to stay in our safe places, not shouting, not interfering, not risking his dignity, not risking his rage, leaving him alone all those years, not visiting, scarcely calling, could I have done, could I have done and the times saying no when I should have said yes.

Mitch, oh Mitch, don't you think I know, Evangeline hears again her own voice answering. I ask myself did I pray enough, and yet I know it is not because of my much speaking that I am heard (her sister Beatrice, in her own pain, had accused her of this, of failing to beat down the gates of eternity to take her brother out, when his number was called). I ask myself the same foolish kinds of questions. I know they are foolish, yet I find myself asking them again and again.

Don't say nice things, Micheline cries, beseeching. I don't need someone to say it is not my fault. I need someone to tell me the truth.

We have blamed ourselves because, loving him, we could not be perfect for him. Is all.

Is it? Is it? What your heart say, Evangeline?

My heart say, when have we loved enough? When have we not been guilty? But we see in a glass darkly, never face to face. Not even our own heart we ever fully know, much less another person's. We do the best we can, and the best we can is broken. We live by mercy, and endure by grace, Mitch.

Can those cancel out judgement? Like the dwarf-child, Micheline beats her feet on the floor, her wailing now a mute sound like a kitten's.

They must. Otherwise I cannot comfort you, for then there is no comfort to be had.

In the end, it is Avette's guilt that speaks for them all.

The screen, calibrating memory, shifts and shifts again.

'An is so it go, Auntie, same so,' Avette is saying, the words muffled between sobs. 'This time, I don't tell you a lie.'

'Of course, my child, of course.' The woman in the impossible clothes and pins, tassels and plaques, shakes her head gently at the young girl, but her own face is wet, streams falling and glistening in the grooves between wrinkles, like a crumpled cloth on which snails have crawled.

'Is not just that I know, the whole time, what was going on. Is that I don't stand up in court for him, and that is how the man go free.' The compulsion to rehearse again her confession, the haunting of years, holds her tongue in thrall, over and over again, until her aunt (who was not grey then, but carnival-royal in reds, purples, golds, tassels, phylacteries and pins) sits beside her, draws her near and, bending her own forehead to the young girl's, weeps and comforts as she can. This Evangeline has lived in many places. On the side of a glass mountain. On a nail-coloured sea. In this forest, where the house has been grown over. She has seen a great many things. Even this morning, breaking through the overgrowth to look again at the receding town and district, she found prawns on the ground, breathing the open air as they walked up from the sea. Once upon a time this would have been impossible. But she knows with the passage of time that all things, including letting go, are possible.

The girl bends down to the ground and picks up a package which she thrusts towards her aunt. Worn brown paper, bruised with sweat and the handling of hands. Evangeline takes the parcel.

'I take it back,' the young girl says. 'I couldn't bear for her to have it, in the end.'

'Oh, there was no need,' Evangeline murmurs, shaking out the beautiful skirt. 'No need. Oh, you should have let your mother keep it.'

It is the skirt she (who was not a grey woman then, but a woman dressed in robes of gold, scarlet and purple) bought for the girl to testify in the courtroom, when the girl, stalling, wanting to escape, said she had nothing suitable to wear on a formal occasion.

'But I couldn't go, Auntie, you understand I couldn't go, don't you? I loved Daddy, but he was dead and gone. My mother begged me to spare her disgrace, and maybe they woulda send her to jail too, thinking she agree to it, and you always said, Auntie, you always said, we must look after the living.'

The grey woman remembers the dreadfully scarred woman dressed in the beautiful skirt she had bought for the scarred woman's daughter, the scarred woman watching her with empty eyes across the courtroom benches. She no longer wonders why the scarred woman is wearing this beautiful skirt to make herself look beautiful, and yet does not cover her face, which is no longer a face, for the scars and keloids have almost erased it. She no longer wonders why the scarred woman chose to borrow this skirt, whether it was possession or mockery or atonement, or defiance or hate or a message of longing in code.

The scarred woman was scarred by her own hand, an act of mysterious desperation committed after the death of her husband and the arrest of her lover, both, so that no one knows for which of them – or was it for either of them? – that she slashed her own throat, breasts and wrists, wielding the razor again and again, until her neighbour found her, a wild woman screaming at the sight of her own face in a dreadful mirror shattered on the floor of a blood-soiled room.

She had angered her family by saying hello to the scarred woman, after the trial was over. The scarred woman looked through her and walked away.

'You always said, we must look after the living.' The child has given her own words back to her.

'Yes, in truth, we are given this grace, to look after the living.'

She remembers the rest of what she used to say, to those who came to her laden down with the guilt of death, the death of friends they could not have saved but their hearts said they should have saved, of relatives they had forgiven too late and felt that somehow, in some obscure working of the stars, their lack of forgiving had caused this death. 'My dear, that is pure foolishness. No one is punished for somebody else's sin. We cannot bring back the dead. But we can ask forgiveness of God and the living, for the things we have done and not done, or been and not been. We can pledge to do better each time. To make amends when it is in our power to do it. That is our life story. In the meantime, the dead must be buried. Once and for all, we must allow those who have passed on their rest, not keep on digging them up for new duppy story. Only the dead keep on burying the dead.' She remembers the long feral scream that once fled from a man's head at the lightning shaft of this injunction, and afterwards the long sleep.

But I myself have had no rest, she thinks to herself, her heart flooded with guilt at what she now sees as her own fraud. I keep burying the dead over and over, because my heart will not be comforted from the thought that I failed my brother, or he would not have died. A violent death at the end of a long saga of pain to which you have been privy is not the same as a death by accident, or illness, or in one's bed from old age. It completely reorders the world of knowing, it makes you struggle with the truths you have believed and known.

Evangeline studies the bent head gravely, without answering. She knows the terror and confusion of a young girl and how easily these feelings harden into caked salt over a grown woman's eyes. How weeping can make a seeing person blind. 'I think that you feel, as you felt then, that it was your duty to go,' she says at last, gauging the girl's thoughts. 'That you owed him the truth. And that you didn't owe your mother a lie.'

'Auntie, what you saying? That I owed my dead stepfather my mother's life? Auntie, mi modda cut up herself! My mother was going kill herself!'

'I'm just saying, you made a choice that has not given you peace. You are still haunted by the thought that you should have gone.'

'Auntie, yu si mi now? I can live with a lot of things. But not killing mi modda. I not killing mi modda.'

'Still it is the truth that will set you free. You won't be free until you tell the truth,' the grey woman says, as she has said all the other times before.

Her heart is breaking with pity. She thinks what a terrible thing for any mother to do to her child, to buy her child's conscience with love. She wonders with grief about her sister-in-law who could not stand her own face, or her own heart. She has not seen the scarred woman in years. The last time she had tried to visit, the scarred woman shut the door in her face. Afterwards when they met on a crowded street, the scarred woman ignored her greeting and crossed to the other side, as if afraid the grey woman would step unforgivably out of bounds. And her handwritten letter was returned unopened. Finally the scarred woman went away, to another country, where she was not known. Now all Evangeline offers are prayers.

'Why you come to see me again, then, Avette?'

'I just want you to understand, Auntie. I couldn't bear for you not to understand.'

'My love, I understood long ago. And I never had you up in my heart. Is God you must talk to, Avette. Is God will give you what you need.'

The girl cries and cries, without answering. Evangeline waits for her to be still. The girl shivers and is quiet at last. Evangeline kisses the swollen face and wipes it with a cloth dipped in cold water.

Then, 'Come,' she says, rising, holding out her hand.

But Avette takes off like a kite.

In a way, had they not all acted, or not acted, for the same kinds of reasons as the young girl had? Each of them acting in their different ways on behalf of the living. Each uncertain if they were right, or wrong. Dear God, forgive us, not as if he was dead and to be forgotten. Not as if he was annihilated from existence. Just that he had passed out of this sphere where we weep and tend to those who remain. Still, uncertain if they were right or wrong.

Mitch in her arms, weeping. 'And afterwards, when he was gone, not even justice. When the sloppy prosecution said they had no evidence, and the naked man went free, we did not even pursue a civil case, might not a civil case have stood for the record, and the justice, even if it never brought him back?'

It was what they all, except she, Evangeline, said in the beginning. She had understood enough to know that without Avette they didn't stand a chance. Faced with the choice of saving or breaking the girl who had remained silent on behalf of her mother, they turned to her, and she had said, let be, and is haunted by that decision forever.

From the beginning, long before she knew it, she was drawn into protecting Avette. From the day that child waited at the crossroads, when I didn't come, because the planes could not fly, and she gave the message, the true story, to Beatrice instead. Message that she carried in her hands like an offering, or a cry for absolution, because she knew how soon she was going to run away from telling it in the courtroom where Pete would need her to tell it.

Perhaps the child hoped that with the true story in my hands, I could make blood out of stone, or speech out of no voice, and somehow make the courts understand the truth, in the one witness's absence. 'Ah, but, my dear,' she thinks, 'I was born in an airplane, not a manger.'

So the girl made these excuses, one after another: I have no dress to wear, I have no memory of what happened, it was this way, no, this was the way, interminably, like a stunned, naïve child, and then, more cunningly, like someone who has grown up overnight in a hard and terrible place, a country of constant murderings, and no justice: I fear to go, Auntie, I fear for my life. But the police, long savvy, would not accept Evangeline's plea to place the young girl in witness protection. 'She trying to fool you, Mummy,' they said, pitying, ceitfulling, calling her by the name of respect for women of her age, even those who had not had children. 'She wiser than you, Mummy. The statement she give us, can't put her in any jeopardy. Who is going to kill her for saying the prisoner acted in self-defence? The prisoner? Or your family?'

And she, too stricken in her grief to understand, to want to understand, asking what must have seemed to Avette the most foolish of questions, until the girl took her heels in her hand and fled, and could not be found, and her perjured statement stood in court beside the naked man's plea of self-defence and her scarred mother's testimony that she wasn't there, nor her daughter. And the grey woman finally understood what the police sergeant, pitying, had tried to tell her. She was the wise one, and yet she had so foolishly failed to understand so simple a thing. In the end it was her youngest sister, Peaches, who stood up in court and shouted the truth that Avette had told to Beatrice to tell Evangeline (in a time when she wore royal colours, before she was grey), Peaches, who was put out of the court for disrupting the peace, and her testimony refused as hearsay, and after it was over people who were there came to her and said, we believe you, but this is a time of fear, a bad time, and people are afraid, for fear has cut out our tongues.

Afterwards Peaches cursed them for accepting Evangeline's counsel, and aroused their guilt and shame. Beatrice tried to bring them back to their self-respect by saying it is true, we had to let it go, for Mumsy's sake. Beatrice, like Avette, speaking on behalf of her mother, their mother who had cried out against the thought of a long pursuit of litigation without evidence. 'Oonu tink all a dat can bring back mi son? Lef me be! Oh Christ, lef me be!', their mother who'd had enough to bear already with their father suffering from the degenerative brain disease that left him scarcely aware of what was going on, much less to give support, their mother who'd had her son buried in the public cemetery and not the family plot, though no Pointy had ever been buried elsewhere before, not even Tramadol dying in the US of A, Tramadol whom she had sent her estranged son to bring back home, because no Pointy had ever been buried away from home, and yet she could not bear it that her son should be buried in the family plot, to remind her of grief she would rather forget. Beatrice said, it is true, let be, our mother could not endure it.

But Evangeline knows, without being told, how, in the intervening years, they have each died (at first daily, and then in snatches, in sudden moments of remembering, on anniversaries of his death, perhaps even his wedding), because they had found no way to heal themselves of the terror of feeling they had abandoned their brother in his lifetime, loved him too little, done for him too little, had him up in their hearts too long, made excuses to stay in their safe places, not shouted, not interfered, not risked his dignity, not risked his rage to keep him alive, and she knows, without being told, that sometimes they feel they would have been vindicated if they had ignored her advice and gone after Avette, to bring her back, to vindicate their brother, to bring back for him the justice of truth. She does not know what else she could have counselled. But she fears in her heart that her siblings have blamed her for closing this gate of redemption, which she thinks is no gate at all, and she feels guilty for thinking her siblings could think such a thing, she, the elder sister, whose prophesyings and visions, injunctions and rebukes have held them in thrall, resentment, love and fear, who knew where the scarred woman's daughter was hiding but would not tell her sisters or her brothers, but told them rather to let be, lest the girl be broken in pieces and still would not speak.

Maryam's daughter had come to her as a penitent to the confessional, once, at the crossroads, and then again, and yet again, before fleeing into hiding, each time bringing one more piece of her broken gifts of confession, trying to mend what, without the truth, could not be made whole. The grey woman knows how little the space can be between one person's experience of guilt and another's, and between one motive of rescue and another, when either way it is a life that is at stake. Still her heart is torn by the longing to find again her sisters and brothers, from whom she was separated when she was young, for she knows they think of her somewhat as a stranger.

Whenever she thinks of these things she is burdened by the guilt of her own failings, by the what ifs and imperfections of love, and moreover the guilt that is carried by those who preach and warn in the streets, keep vigil at the crossroads, rebuke in the churches, exhort in the schools, lambast the idlers, wash the indigent, nurse the sick, call on God's name, all the time haunted by the fear of their own hubris and the fear of self-service. She thinks of the terror of speaking in the name of truth, in case one is mistaken, and thinking of these things she prays, Lord have mercy, Christ have mercy.

In such moments she longs for the comfort she has given to others. It comes to her in snatches of dwarf-song, when the curtains of self-doubt are pulled back without her doing and the past seems to roll itself up in a scroll.

'You carried our hurt for us, even in this, all those years, inside your chest like that?' Micheline bursts out, speaking to the virtual screen.

153

'We hated you, you know. You know that, don't you? You were always so right. It is dreadful to be exposed to someone who is always so right.'

'Did you think I was right not to force Avette to testify?' Evangeline asks, her voice tinged with both longing and irony.

She doubts her certain truths, even as I doubt the uncertain ones that keep me mending the story, fitting things back in their assigned places, Micheline thinks in amazement.

'But you couldn't have, could you?' Micheline watches her sister's face, studying how it flickers on the screen. Extreme emotion sometimes prevents the picture from staying still. 'I mean, she was pretty determined, wasn't she?'

'That's not an answer,' Evangeline says, and in her voice Micheline hears her own cry for the relief of a singular truth. 'I felt that if you all hated me then, it was because you felt I was horribly wrong.'

She cannot give the singular answer; it is all too complicated. 'No, not wrong. But worse than right. Righteous. Insufferably,' she quips.

They both laugh, but there are tears in her sister's eyes. 'I think we hated you that time because we felt helpless without you,' Micheline says. 'We were too stunned to know what to do, and we hoped you would, as you always did. You always seemed to be on such good terms with God, with Christ. But nothing you could have said would have given us any surcease, not then. We each had to deal with our own feelings of guilt on our own. One doesn't really get to the confessional until the tail-end of a long journey, when you've pretty much worked out the basics in your own mind already, does one? Maybe absolution is just another word for confirmation. Of what a person knows in her heart of hearts to be true.'

Her sister is silent. When she answers at last her words seem irrelevant. 'So strange to be watching my own face talking to someone else. My words leaving my mouth and turning themselves into print while I speak. Like I'm a virtual person, not real at all. Technology is something, ehn?'

'Until you helped me see things differently, see God in the picture, I used to feel unreal every time I had to make a terrible choice. Like the universe had taken over and I was just being pulled along, in opposite directions, by forces I can't control. Funny, that's the image that always comes to my mind when I think of people being drawn and quartered, in medieval times.'

'Still, it was a lot of blood,' Evangeline says, smiling a little.

'Yes. And body pieces. So it couldn't have been so unreal, could it? It's really horrible of me to think of unreality and such a horrifically real experience in the same breath, isn't it?'

'Not really. It's one and the same.'

'Yes, I suppose it is. Now I think about it. Not to feel that one has choice. Or control. One feels so unreal, so irrelevant. And yet it is the choices that tear us to pieces.'

'Yes.' Evangeline knows how often the choices in life are between equal forces of conscience, or forces of conscience that seem in the moment of choice to be equal. *We make the choice we believe we can live with at the moment we make it, having asked for guidance, and trust God to cover our mistakes.* She thinks, as countless others have thought before and since, that if there had been no God, she would have invented God, for how else to bear the burden and risk of choice?

She prays for the young girl, Avette, who is now a grown woman, for she thinks neither the young girl nor the woman has had rest. She thinks of the stories she has heard, of a wild girl following in the footsteps of her mother, and, latterly, more. Stories of prostitution, hauntings and carousels at the piers, where the sailors and the cruise boats come in, where the fleeing people push their own boats out to sea, off the island's edge to an imagined safer shore. How long she had herself haunted these piers, searching, hoping to bring the child back to peace, but always the girl eluded her, until finally she stopped searching, and now she waits, as she always has, even for her own heart to still, believing.

The grey woman has had many secrets and thoughts that her sisters have not known. She had never told her sisters that she felt relief when Beatrice, too, said, let be, for our mother's sake, dissuading them from pursuing the civil case anyhow, without Avette. She has never told them that her relief was not for her mother's sake but on her own account, the account of her own fear of suffering, the suffering of her siblings' rejection; the long terror of the courtroom again and again, in an effort that would probably be wasted, leaving in its wake a handful of bitterness, like ashes; and the pain which in dreams and visions she would undergo for all of them. She does not tell them how often she has wondered how much of her 'let be' was for the most selfish of reasons, the right decision for the wrong reasons, whether her actions had been derelict in the end.

The dwarf-child is keening in the next room. The sound shocks the sisters into silence because it is not a sound he has uttered before. It is not the long ululation of his happiness nor the feral howling he emits when he feels that the world is broken and will never be mended in the thousand years of a child's life. It is a sound between the two, a broken sobbing such as a child utters in sight of a beautiful thing that it wants to grasp, that is loving him back quite fiercely, but is separated from him behind an open fence. In this memory within the telling of a memory, Evangeline's face vanishes from the screen as she exits rapidly to see what is wrong.

We belong to the same blood but I never had so little skin, Mitch is saying to Mitch, watching her words imprint on the voracious screen. I can make for myself any number of skins at the drop of a hat, and change them all out again just as fast. I guess that's why I'm the writer and she the priest – though she knows Evangeline would say, priests are called, not born. She is frightened to think she has not known her sister at all. She wonders how it has been with Beatrice and Peaches, and the younger ones, Truck, Vicki and Davidow. She wonders with deep regret, how life had been for Tram. Perhaps those of us who grew up so close to each other, in the same house, who were never sent away, didn't know each other so well either. Perhaps it is no different between us who stayed at home. We take closeness for granted, mistaking proximity for intimacy.

She tries not to think of Pete but she does, painfully, for isn't it all because of Pete? The one they have known best is Pete, and only because of his diaries, which he did not give them permission to read. We have come to know Pete through a betrayal of trust, raiding his private thoughts after he was dead. In life, who is able to read the book of anyone's thoughts? It is as Evangeline has said. We see through a glass only darkly. For that reason alone I hope we can all forgive ourselves.

And in the same way that one can have in one's possession an artifact of great value and not know its value until a chance encounter with a connoisseur, in the moment of her sister's confessions she suddenly realizes something of great importance about Pete's diaries, that Pete had never written a bad word about any of them; indeed, in the notebooks that he used to wrestle out his anguish of spirit, he mentioned his siblings so little, that she can only think they were not in his mind a source of trouble or conflict. We do not wrestle with the relationships that bring us peace. Mostly he mentioned Evangeline, when he thought of seeking advice. That has to count for something, Mitch thinks. Surely that says he never felt there was anything to forgive us for.

But that was before we let him die. The thought leaps unbidden, not letting her easily go free.

'But I am already free.' Ashamed of herself for refusing the grace that the thought of her brother's diaries afforded, she hits back fiercely at the cruel thought, determined not to go down that road again. 'We did the best we could. The best we could was broken. Take care of the living. By Christ's grace.' And she clings fiercely in her heart to her sisters, overtaken by a fierceness of love so painful, that she cries out aloud, bringing her sister back into the room.

'What's wrong?'

'Nothing,' Micheline says radiantly. 'Nothing at all. What happened to him?'

'He was trying to patch himself with skin.'

'What?'

'Not real skin. He downloaded some so-called flesh colour off the net and was trying to make it work on his body. It turned him indigo.'

'But he has never done that before!' She is half-distressed, half-amused.

'No.' Evangeline herself cannot help smiling. 'It's the excitement of knowing he'll soon be given a skin. He was acting out for himself what it might be like, but when he turned blue he got scared that the

doctors might not be able to give him a skin like other people's after all.'

'He thought they might give him blue skin.' Micheline's lips are still twitching.

'Or green, like Cybermonster.'

'How is he now?'

'I cleaned him up and told him a story. He fell asleep.'

'Will he get nightmares?'

'He doesn't, usually. He's okay once he says his prayers.'

'Not haunted by ghosts.'

'No, not haunted by ghosts.'

Ghosts, like the denizens of a box opened in the annals of antiquity, which came with an injunction not to open. Unleashed all those millennia ago, they have kept flitting in and out of brain and body cells, playing havoc with the human genome. Among the things Evangeline had never told her sisters is how she is not allowed to forget the naked man, the naked man who killed her brother, how the naked man does not allow himself to be forgotten. The naked man confronts her in her prayers. For a long time she could not think about him at all, because she could not bring herself to think of him with mercy, grace, or love, and she could not tell whether her heart yearned for justice or revenge.

But the naked man is naked because he wishes to be seen; the naked man will not be pushed to the periphery or viewed like a ghost on the edge of an eyelid or the corner of an eye; if she says, 'Maryam', the naked man comes; if she calls in her prayers the generations of her brothers' children, the naked man comes; the naked man is insistent, exigent, rounding on her suddenly in corners, saying look, look, look at me, look, showing slyly, with a spectral grin, the mark on his forehead.

Inch by inch the grey woman ceded him ground.

She prayed against him for justice, and would not look at his face. But the naked man would not be denied; with the steadfast assurance of those who have gone over the edge, he is sure she will give him his desire, a companion to go with him in his long vagabondage over the earth, and he is not taking closed eyes for an answer. Inch by inch, the grey woman ceded him ground. Now, he has taken up space in two ventricles of her heart, which have balanced themselves like scales, one weighing justice, the other, the mantras of grace. She does not pray for the naked man to be well, or happy, or free. She prays for the naked man to return to the point of choice, the memory of choice, the memory of the knife; she imagines the naked man driven down long corridors of flight by the vengeance of the Holy Ghost, at his tail, like a comet, a trailer of dreams, visions, incantations, predictions, prophesyings, judgements, exhortations, mercies, rebukes, his own nakedness, his own wound, a man and a posse of furies herded by implacable grace to the bare feet of Christ. She dreams of him handing himself over to justice, and again, like a slideshow, him preaching on piazzas and street corners, laden with a cross, paying back the life he has taken. Sometimes her heart, in which one ventricle, the one carrying the most blood, is thicker than the other, sometimes her heart produces, like a quick camera with a flash, an image of blood: she sees the naked man die violently, cry vainly to a knife-wielder for mercy. She knows her heart to be two-faced, and she speaks to her heart, let be, let be. She thinks that any of these things that she dreams may happen, or all, or none, but she thinks that God is just; she thinks this in a way that is visceral, and real, and she instructs the stripped rooms of her heart, let be, let be.

Her heart is complicated; it has little interest in the issues of physical death; it is haunted by visions of heaven and hell. Knowing this, the naked man taunted her, once, willing himself to be herded not to an ultimate mercy but to the place of the damned, for what can atone for a life but another life? (And indeed, she thinks, you must not be allowed to forget that you took another man's life, without good reason; you must not rest in it, for what can atone for a life but another life?)

There is heaven and there is hell and I do not know my brother's destiny (this Evangeline prays for the dead) for I am not God, but this I do know, two deaths do not make a life, so I am not giving you what you want, I am not Prince Hamlet, I am not going there with you.

'No,' she tells the naked man, who leers at her, daring her to touch the mark on his forehead. 'I am not going over that edge, or letting you go over without shouting.' She knows that to entertain the thought of him going over that edge is to go over there with him too. 'No way, José, I am going nowhere such with you.' He never tried that again.

As she calls the naked man back with her prayers, she sees that she is not the only one in flight; pursued, she has also been pursuing; the naked man is ceding her ground. Gradually, over the years, the face he is hiding is exposed, beneath the mark on his forehead. It is the face of terror, a man's terror of his own heart, and beseeching. It stuns her to think that the naked man, like a twin, has taken up as many acres of ground as her brother in her heart, and she cannot imagine how many acres her brother, and she, her sisters, her mother, her father, her brother's brothers, and her brother's son, have taken up in his.

Micheline stares numbly at the thing that has appeared on the computer screen. She glances over at the image of her sister's face, but Evangeline's face is absorbed, blind, completely unaware. Beyond the room is the open French door through which the cyber-screen has caught in its frame a section of the massed hedge that the children had burst through not so many hours before. She can see, as clearly as if he were standing in front of her, the imprint of the man's face on the shivering hedge, the same face rigid with beseeching and terror, that Evangeline had described. Except that Evangeline hadn't. You didn't say any of this, she thinks over and over, and over again, but the image and the words about the naked man turning, in answer to Evangeline's shout, 'I will not let you go without shouting!' do not go away; they remain bright on the screen as if they had projected out of Evangeline's brain, except that Evangeline did not speak and they have been written.

'Retro me, you dirty bastard,' Mitch swears through gritted teeth in her mind. 'I am no Evangeline. I hope somebody chop up your raas. I don't care where God send you afterwards, so long as right here in this life you feel hell.' But even as her mind utters this curse, she calls it back, feeling herself slipping over the edge of horror from

which, in her sister's words of hard comfort, she has sought and found reprieve. She calls the words back and whispers, 'Mercy. Grace. Forgive. Even as you are forgiven, forgive.' Even if you know that because God is just and that wicked man must get him punishment. She watches the image disappear from the shaking hedge where a moment ago it had imprinted. She has never retained the man in her heart before and when she has thought of him she has thought only of justice and vengeance. Now, it seems, if Evangeline did not speak those last words, it must be that he has dislodged himself from her sister's confessions and lodged himself like a grain of sand in some lobe of her mind, predicting a long twinship of irritation that will either mangle her heart or rub her raw to an infinite pearl. For a moment she is furious again with her sister, whose confessions now stick to her writer's susceptible hands like the incontinent grain of sand in an oyster's lip, or iron pyrites on metal. 'Mercy. Grace. Forgive,' she whispers again.

'Yes,' Evangeline says, thinking her sister, like Avette, is giving her own words back to her. But Micheline is saying them for herself.

The grey woman has weathered many storms, is strong, is imperial, thinks easily and naturally of love, yet she knows to herself that only in this, a violent death in a soiled room, has her heart truly been tested. She has lived in many places in her heart, yet she knows that if she were to take a clew of thread, she would be hard put to find or return from its lower rooms or the violence that they guard. But this Evangeline is patient, and has waited for her heart, as she has waited for Beatrice, and Micheline, and Avette, and Maryam, and the dwarf-child, and where everything ends, and then begins.

★

'Come.' It is the dwarf child tugging her impatiently back to himself, from where she has gone in her mind to the memory of the long night remembering with Micheline. 'Come.' He wants to play, but has accepted that he is not allowed, without supervision or his harness. She helps him on with the harness, working around his impatiently seething hands that get in the way as he tries to make his accoutrement happen faster. She touches every vibration of the small, over-tender body through

161

the radar of her fingertips, feeling its greed, the greed for life, race through the vesicles. Like every other child, he yearns to run, climb, dance, shout, scream, fling something at the sun and bring even one star falling down.

The harness protects him from the bruising that if he fell would kill him in an instant, a child falling to earth without skin. They call him the dwarf-child because of his harness, which makes him look like a man in a moon suit, or a huge beetle, or a cyborg. He cannot go outside without it, otherwise he will die of allergies, or the sun. The harness plays tag with his membrane, tracking each nuance of light and heat and cold and darkness, regulating his response to each.

She sits under the trees and watches him climb, shimmy (for dancing), bake mudpies which he feeds to the endless companions that shut her out as soon as they burst through the undergrowth into the clearing to play. Against these also he wrestles, wins potato sack-races (the only kind he can run, with his delicate, unformed feet), plays marbles and chess and when they cry, condescends once in a while not to let them lose. Tired of battle, he switches personae with the silver speed of invention; sits them down in rows in his sun-filled classroom on the grass, teaches, admonishes, rebukes, waving a stern headmaster's, or headmistress's, finger towards their faces. They must sit hushed and listening, saying only 'ooh' and 'aah' and 'yes, teacher', 'say what, teacher?' under the spell of his tellings, unless he asks them a question, which they must answer right or be sent disgraced to a corner, because clearly they were not listening, or did not care. They must all borrow his voice, singing out their answers and their repentance in his unearthly beautiful song. This playtime by himself is not like the adventure of yesterday, when the village children came and he had to answer their questions. Here he is king, here he calls all the shots.

He reads history, and likes old books. He likes to read the old books in the old way, not on his cyber-slate but the printed pages of the museum pieces she has kept in her library, tomes that smell of must and mystery. Sometimes his companions are his subjects, and he their king. Reading Lewis Carroll, he

162

tells them it is wicked to cut off heads, he will never cut off heads, but they must be obedient to the king. Then, quickly bored, he organizes a rebellion against the king. Later on, in quick or belated solicitude and compassion, he hides them in the shade of the undergrowth and feeds them mudpies for lunch, as he has done for breakfast, and will again for their dinner. They must imagine and thank him for the eggs, chocolate, multigrain, fried plantains, cowfoot, callaloo and banana. He himself cannot eat by the normal channels, but must be fed through the tube in his side, at small intervals throughout the day. He does not know how food tastes. Yet he is fascinated by the anatomy of eating. Quickly converting his classroom into a space hospital, he lays his patients out on beds and conducts surgical experiments on their throats, their lips, their intestines. Later he will show her the notes he has written, taking medical histories in his white coat.

'This is Dr Pointy-Morris. Don't move. Don't be scared. I am not going to hurt you. I am going to cut your throat here, and here, make a small incis— Momma how do you spell incis— the incis word? Hush, don't let them hear, they will think I didn't really go to medical school. Incis-ion. Yes. Make a small incision. Then I will open it wider. I'm afraid I will have to open it wider. Cut out a piece of your – th... – oh, bother, can't spell it, a piece of your leg, and make a tongue, like this, see, like this, and you will be able to talk. Better than the space hospital. Better. See, I did not hurt you. Did I hurt you? Of course not, I did not hurt you. Tell God I did not hurt you. Tell God, thanks. Thank you, God, the doctor fixed me better, he did not hurt me.' For the past few days, he has ended his play with monologues like this, working through his anxiety and his hope, while she watches and prays.

And for the two hours or so of these unseen friends' pres-ence, he ignores her completely, except in the rare moments when he needs her to spell a word, or corroborate a piece of information, or help him invent a new lie. She sits anxious and enchanted under the sound of his song, the low, then high, melodious keening that skims the tops of the trees and loops to the other side, where the district once was. When they are all exhausted he comes back to her, all hers again, trailing pieces of himself in tatters, his eyes gleaming and satisfied.

She knows them all by heart now, even though every day he invents them differently, anew. Day before yesterday they were Sten and Patrice whom he has had to rebuke, because they are too inseparable, and will not play with the others unless made to do so. Must not be selfish. Karaoke who likes to tell stories but never remembers them right. How can you be a storyteller if you have no memory, Momma? She cheats, she just makes up things as she goes along. Do you think the space hospital can give her a new brain, so she doesn't lie so much? Claudette with blue shoes, she will climb eleven steps. Derek who wants to come and live with us, but I told him no. Derek is too bad. Cyril who is never satisfied – sit, sit, Cyril. Wait. Be patient, don't grab. Pauline who never says her prayers, and does bad things behind the grass.

Smiling behind her hand, she dares not ask what the bad thing is that Pauline does behind the grass. She is glad that today, after the abandonment by their real counterparts yesterday that made him cry, he is content to rule and punish, exhort and forgive. This tells her his rage has not taken him over; he is whole again. Indeed, she sees with amusement that he has incorporated yesterday's banter into his play.

'Look, boy, I will burst boil in your face! I can make it fly further than you can pee!'

'Dwarf-boy can't pee far!'

'Nor girl!'

'Move off, boy! Your thing hanging down, like spout! Girl don't need that.'

'Shhh. Stop talking rudeness, Derek. Stop talking rudeness, Pauline. Momma can hear you!'

His emotional and play-lives have not kept pace with his mental dexterity; in these, he is barely three years old.

In the beginning he used to ask her, 'Momma, where did all the children go? Why don't they come any more?'

It is one of the questions he no longer asks. He brings the children back for himself, under these new names.

He is happiest in their company, but he also loves the days

when she dyes cloth, which she does in the old-fashioned way. He loves to help her mix the glowing colours and hang the bright panels of linen and calico on the clothesline, laughing with all his might at the way the tints shadow his membrane, in shifting colours like an array of gems that ripple faster than the mercury in an hourglass. 'Look, Momma, I'm a rainbow!' and he wants to spin forever in circles of glee in the bright sunlight, but she has to take him inside from too much exposure. This makes him angry, and he becomes hopelessly naughty, breaking or throwing down everything his fragile hands can lift, screaming in that terrible feral howl that has made the district afraid of his origins. A spectral child. A Whooping Boy child. A sign more *aweful* than the Hecatonchires at the dawn of the world's first sin.

She is constantly astonished at her nephew Davidow, Davvy's affinity with the dwarf-child. Davvy will listen without flinching to the dwarf-child's howl as well as his song, making music of both. He seems to hear at a decibel level higher than anyone else, so that he is able to calibrate each wave of sound into lines of words and accompanying instruments. Percussion, drums. Over and under the flutes, violins, cymbals and bass guitar. The long drawn-out cry of the blue saxophone. Life and colour and death and darkness. Lyrics and sounds that have made him famous. A gritty, haunting sound, Davvy's music, which in his interviews he has attributed not to the dwarf-child but to the journeys he has made up and down the face of the island and the museum of song in which he spends long hours listening and scoring. The dwarf-child has been taught the names of Davvy's mentors by heart, and sings them sometimes in a string of sound, beating time with his hands. Skatalites, Bob Marley and the Wailers, Toots and the Maytals, Chalice, Third World, Rita and the I-Threes, Buju, Beenie, Elvis, Tiger, Mavado, Queen Ifrica, Townes, Mahalia, Whitney, Jimmy, Judy, Paul and Art, MJ, Ziggy, Nina, Nana, Pluto, Otis, Aretha, Louis, Billie, Masekela, the Burning Spear.

Micheline often laughs in astonishment at this child's memory. 'Is there anything he forgets?' She throws up her hands, laughing. 'You have to be careful with this one. Can't talk secrets in his hearing.'

'Auntie Micheline, no cup nuh break, no coffee nuh t'row 'way.'

'What the Dickens you know about any of that?'

The dwarf-child runs away laughing. Davvy clips him on the side of the head as he passes. He's the only one who is not afraid to romp a little rough with the dwarf-child.

Mitch loves the dwarf-child fiercely, but it is with Davvy he has a connection, as if they have come from the same place together.

This evening when the grey woman says 'Come', the dwarf-child is unprotesting about going to bed, as he has not been in a long time. His whole being is folded tight around the promise of Monday, when the doctors will come to take him away to make him almost a normal child. She thinks of her sister Beatrice, the fiercely stay-at-home one, grumbling, 'All they life black people have to be migrating to survive. And look now it gone so bad, this one migrating to outer space.' It would not bother B at all that the dwarf-child has no skin, and no marking for skin in his DNA, so no one knows what race he really is. 'What that got to do with anything? Don't is black people raise him? So him well black.'

Evangeline answers her sister in her mind, comforting her about their going away. 'Outer space not all that far, when you think about it, B. The chains that hold us to this place where our dead lie deep, always pull us back.'

'Or not.' B's voice in her head.

Evangeline doesn't answer that. 'We can give thanks he was selected in the lottery. And that he has no phenotype to identify him black so they could roll the dice again and choose some other child in his place. Because how could we have afforded to pay for this treatment?'

'Chuups.' B kissing her teeth. 'You have to look at the other side of freeness. So they can do dangerous experiment with impunity.'

Evangeline thinks about other deeds that are done with impunity, and this time again she does not answer her sister.

But the dwarf-child is unaware and unconcerned about Beatrice's things. All night in his dreams the bush-bush shakes with the motion of flying. He sleeps soundlessly until morning.

A drone and a shout from the clearing wake them. It is Micheline and Davvy disembarking from their silver cyberchute, Micheline and Davvy come to spend the last day before the grey woman and the dwarf-child leave. The dwarf-child leaps up and, with sleep still in his eyes, runs heedlessly towards the sound, drawn by the shining silver ship that has landed on the grass, and his aunt and father walking towards him, their arms outstretched.

And the grey woman, tumbling after, equally sleepy-eyed, is lifted free by the sound of their laughter and the dwarf-child's fluting song.

V

SEED

In the green-dark room in the bejewelled house with its garden rich and ruinate, Micheline hears time ticking down like the drift in a mercury clock. She can hear the mercury slide, slickly, as if she had ants' ears. Hung in this capsule of time where everything else in the world has gone still, she watches again her sisters' and her own confessions unroll on the screen, on her stunned mind and she thinks how close and yet how separated they have been from each other – Tram whom they have thought strange, and Pete who in his strange loves had locked himself away from his sisters, both because he was a man and his sisters were women, and because he was Pete and that was the way he was; Beatrice, Peaches, she, all of them chained in the helplessness of their love; Evangeline whom they have both loved and hated and kept apart from because of her exigent faith that made them all feel guilty, Evangeline whom they had never thought could cry, whose tears are the last and most fluent in this book of tears – and why not, for had she not carried the burden of separations more than them all, the one who was sent away young (and moreover in our country it is hard to be the eldest sister and a seer, especially one born in the sky, in a sac, as if one had no skin)? All of them had been broken by the helplessness of love, bearing the one burden side by side without knowing; they have all been, as Evangeline would say, they have all been like Joseph, the one who was separated from his brethren, upon all whose heads, by way of healing, I, Micheline now pray 'the blessings of heaven above, the blessings that lie under, the blessings of the breasts and of the womb, and of the utmost bounds of the everlasting hills.' That, Micheline tells herself smiling, has to be a prayer of faith indeed, for even at this moment the deep is polluted beyond measure, the milk of breasts is quite probably cancerous, and the hills fired with greenhouse gases are smoking away.

'You, too, need to absolve yourself,' she tells her sister Evangeline again. 'You give yourself a hard time. You should get some easement. Talk to someone who will help you, as you have helped us.'

But it is to her, weaver of unstraight truths, that her sister has told her story, face to face. She knows it is no casual choice that was made.

Nevertheless, 'Yes,' Evangeline says. 'Tomorrow.'

Tomorrow, days before they must take the dwarf-child for his surgeries, the elder sister will go to see her friend, Jeremy the priest, another of the foolish ones who have refused to flee the lowlands, watching time shift on its bases, yet stubbornly staying, grasping after eternity, as if, Micheline thinks, the violence of their longing can take it by force. 'Somebody has to stay, for those who cannot leave,' is Jeremy's excuse. A lame-footed man in perennially rumpled clothes, not like a priest at all.

All Souls Day, November 2, 2059.
Today Pete has company. All day, starting between last night's second twilight and dawn, his brothers and sisters have made treks across the roadside bridge that was laid over the lake of eyewaters formed from the weeping after his death. Their movements slow and purposeful, they made their way along the narrow paths between headstones to come to the porcelain slab with the simple stone saying 'Peter Evaristo Pointy-Morris, 24 October 1998 –1 August 2047.' A single fat white candle, still whole, as if has been newly placed, burns in a holder by the stone. It gives off a faint smell of cloves. Its light is pale, absorbed in the sheen of the bright day. (Earlier, before the dark broke, there had been many more candles. Their lights, catching the surface of the waters, turned into bent pillars that made the lake an under-water city. Now only the last candle, the dwarf-child's, guards

172

the city). His siblings have brought him flowers; the grave is covered with blooms, among them his favourites, heliconias shaped and plumaged like birds and a trellis of 'stringing' roses – the tiny petunias that still grow wild on the island. As children, we used to string them on grass stems and hang them around our necks like insignias of office, calling ourselves kings. Pete will be pleased that we remembered him not dead but living, Micheline thinks, smiling. She and Pete's son, Davvy, are the only ones left of the long company that has come to say howdy all day. B's children had come visiting from Jerusalem and Barcelona. Poor B. Just like spite, her children were the ones who lived farthest away. Still they had come to say howdy to their uncle. Yes, Pete would be pleased.

'I destroy what was done wrongly against me, I dispel what was done evilly against me.'

What does it mean? It means that the navel-string of Ani will be cut.

'All the ill which was on me has been removed.'

'Huh?' Davvy is staring at her with a puzzled look.

Mitch laughs. 'It's something from the Book of the Dead that your cousin Tram was always quoting.'

'Oh. Yeah?'

'Yeah.'

They are quiet a bit. Davvy is strumming again the strings of his guitar. Mitch beats time with her foot to the music, which begins low and throbbing:

> 'O Jah who live in heaven
> Hallowéd be your name
> Your kingdom come in us
> Your will be done in us
> (as it is in heaven)
> Hallowéd be your name.
> Your bread we need each day
> Hallowéd be your name.
> Your forgiveness now we pray
> Hallowéd be your name.

As we forgive as we forgive
Hallowéd be your name.'

Does he know this was the unfinished prayer on his father's lips, which his grandmother had wanted to pray with her son? We didn't tell him, Mitch realizes. I should tell him, some time.

Davvy shifts on his seat on the plinth and the rhythm shifts with him, the sound now husky and deep as he finishes:

Now Jah -Jah give we wing
Hallowéd be your name.
Now Jah-Jah help we fly
Hallowéd be your name.

Yearning, excoriating, before sliding down again to quiet:

Now Jah-Jah help we fly
Hallowéd be your name.
See Jah-Jah mek we fly
Hallowéd be your name.

As the notes fall softly into the silence around them, Micheline looks out beyond the border of the lake to where the ring of trees cloaks the disappearing town. The trees are still, then tremble, as though a horseman had passed by.

'Is who dat?'

Mitch opens her mouth to answer, then realizes Davvy is not looking at the trees but at the crossroads where a lone figure stands, watching, as it had stood fourteen years before.

'It's a beginning,' Mitch murmurs, as the figure flits and disappears.

CODA

For several months after I read my siblings' accounts of the different ways in which they experienced this tragedy that broke all our hearts over so many years, I was unable to sleep. Their stories haunted me, not because of the anguish relived (all of us relived), but because I knew that there was something missing, which it was my part to find, and I didn't know what it was. In the end I followed my nose, my abiding curiosity about this ridiculous name Pointy, to see where it would take me.

I went to the museum of books, which is located next door to the Global Museum of Songs (the same museum of songs where my nephew Davidow goes to search out forgotten albums). I had promised to leave things alone, but in the end, unsatisfied, I went looking for the point of cleavage, where our family got its wound. I went looking for the meanings and origins of our name.

And found Pointy. From the French pointeau, meaning an engraver's needle, or a timekeeper in a factory, a place where things are made. I found also pont; in South Africa, a river ferry, especially one that is guided by a cable from one bank to another. From the Afrikaans, which is from the Dutch for ferryboat, which is related to the Latin pons, a bridge, from which, in English, pontage, a duty or tax paid for access to a bridge, a price paid, and pontifex, from the Latin pons and fex/facere, made/to make. A pontifex. A bridgemaker. Between the gods and the world. Pontifex Maximus, the high priest, the maker of the highest (most enduring?) bridge. A price paid. For making bridges. Or crossing them.

I already knew that the name, Morris, was also that of a dance. Morris, the name, from English, Scots, Irish and

Welsh, travelling across centuries, times, continents and worlds, from Constantinople to North Africa, to Spain, to Rome, to France, to Britain and finally Jacaranda. Carried above a ship's womb filled with the ravished children of Mother Africa. A ship of names, ledgerdemaining, shimmying, broken at limbo, the place of wounds. Morris, an English and a Scots name, from the Old French Maurice, brought over by the Normans. From the Latin Mauritius, derivate of Maurus, a native of North Africa, and also a name given to many early Christian saints (Pointy's high priest and Morris' saints, meeting, there in the heart of a far country, a legacy of people who fought each other all the time); in Spanish, Moro, as in sarraceno, Saracen, or árabe, Arab, one of many names given to the conquerors of medieval Spain which, in her turn, conquered the island of Jacaranda, Columbus sailing 1494, before it was conquered by the English, Admiral Penn sailing in 1655; also, in medieval and early modern England, a nickname given to any dark-skinned person of that time; whether dark-skinned from Africa, or Turkey, or Mesopotamia, or Jerusalem, did not matter. A black nickname among names. A black hole of a (nick)name. But also an Irish name, from my great-great great grandfather, a version of O' Muirghis, meaning stately, great, or proud (but in my family it was my mother, a Pointy, who was proud; a tourist walking on dry land, the district said). Kindred to the Scottish Muir, kindred to the Welsh Mawr, big, as in too big for your pants, like my suspected-jacket nephew Davidow breaking out of his skin rawboned, or my sister Beatrice of the magnificent overflowing breasts.

A morris dance. A dance of the rural folk in Northern England, a dance danced in costumes on May Day; a dance that had crossed over water from Holland, a country of dykes and dunes, where water is safely fenced, that is, the Flemish *Mouriske dans*; which in its turn crossed over from Old France, where it was danced because of the Moors or after the fashion of the Moors. Whether Moors (meaning black people) of North, or West, or East, or Southern Africa, we do not know. And finally to Jacaranda, Caribbean, where we dance qua-drille, including in our version of this four-cornered dance from Europe a fifth figure, a dance that is not unlike the dance of the Moors, the morrismouriskedans.

I thought to myself when I had found all this out, that though it brought me no nearer to an understanding of any larger significance to our family's wounds, it certainly went a long way, even if only in a purely symbolic sense, towards explaining how so many convolutions, contractions, superstitions, dreams, longings, fragments, fractures, transformations, suturings, breakings, metamorphoses, membranes, silences, flutterings, waters, bridges, obsessions, loves, desperations, faiths, longings, stretches, nobilities, words, have lodged in our mortal bodies and excitable brains. And yet we are only talking about names. Can you imagine if we begin to exhume, or even just think about, bodies, transportations, chains, apprenticeships, indentureships, sailing ships, airplanes, supersonic jets, the sound barrier, the speed of light, submarines, knives, guns, 9/11s, wars, more wars, news of famine, sugarcane, cotton, tobacco, internets, telephones, cables, telescopes, probes, movies, fantasies, oil spills, beached whales, right wing Congresses, betrayal by PNP, betrayal by JLP, betrayal by NOP, hurricanes in London, monsoons in Chicago, wormholes, melanomas, carcinomas, the common cold, space hospitals, the age of consent lowered to ten, Star Trek, Lord of the Rings, Rhodesia, Zimbabwe, South Africa, Las Casas, Sitting Bull, Aborigines, Abraham, Isaac, Sarah, Sojourner Truth, a woman called Moses, nano-games, sky children, genocides, murders, thieveries, 2060, and the long trek from Eden to this place?

I talk too much. I promised my siblings. No amount of talking will shake down Borges' book of sand, or uncouple from my eyes the twinship of hope and tears.

September 18, 2011.

ACKNOWLEDGEMENTS

To my incredibly long-suffering critics, Helen Billy Elm Williams and Carol Brown, my gratitude for your unsparing honesty as critics and your generosity as friends.

The quotations from *The Egyptian Book of the Dead* are from the edition entitled *The Egyptian Book of the Dead: The Book of Going Forth by Day*, ed. Eva Von Dassow in an edition conceived and produced by James Wasserman (San Francisco: Chronicle Books, 1998). The quotation in 'The Change of Life' is from Plate 2 of the 'Introduction to the Hymn to Osiris.' The quotation in 'Seed' is from Chapter 17, Plate 8.

The quotation from Townes Van Zandt's 'To Live is to Fly' is from the audio CD, *Legend: Very Best of Townes Van Zandt*, on the Snapper UK label, 2010.

ABOUT THE AUTHOR

Curdella Forbes was born in the parish of Hanover, the second of nine siblings. Educated in Jamaica and Australia, she taught in high schools and colleges in Jamaica, as well as at the University of the West Indies (UWI), Mona. Between 1990 and 1995 she was Resident Tutor of the UWI School of Continuing Studies in Western Jamaica. She has served in several capacities as an educational consultant and been a member of examining and subject panels for CXC, CAPE Literatures in English and CAPE Communication Studies.

Between stints of professional work in education and academia she has been a newspaper reporter, a factory line worker, and a dog sitter. She has written her books 'in-between spaces' in her full-time jobs of parenting and professional and volunteer work. In 2003 she emigrated to the USA, where she is Professor of Caribbean literature at Howard University in Washington DC. She has published three critically-acclaimed works of fiction, *Songs of Silence* which is currently on the CXC English B syllabus; *Flying with Icarus and Other Stories*, a collection of stories for younger readers; and *A Permanent Freedom* (Peepal Tree 2008). Her stories have appeared in *Bim, Jamaica Journal* and an anthology, *Survivor and Other Stories*, edited by Vivian French. She has also published numerous essays and an academic book, *From Nation to Diaspora: Samuel Selvon, George Lamming and the Cultural Performance of Gender* (University of the West Indies Press, 2005) which won the UWI Award for Best Research Book.

She has read her work by invitation to audiences in Boston, New York, Washington DC and other cities in the USA, and at literary conferences in Trinidad, Puerto Rico, the Dominican Republic and Canada. She was among the Caribbean women writers honoured in the May-October 2008 issue of *Bim*, the first issue dedicated to Caribbean women's writing in *Bim*'s 69-year history. She was an invited writer at Calabash 2003, and a 2005 invited writer in Colgate University's Africana and Latin American Studies Visiting Writers Program.

ALSO BY CURDELLA FORBES

A Permanent Freedom
ISBN: 9781845230616; pp. 195; pub. 2008; price: £8.99

Crossing the space between novel and short fiction, *A Permanent Freedom* weaves nine individual stories about love, sex, death and migration into a single compelling narrative that seizes our imagination with the profound courage, integrity and folly of which the human spirit is capable. Each story surrounds migrant or migrating characters seeking to negotiate life on margins, within silences, in in-between spaces. Through the memory or immediate experience of sexual encounters or love that drives or haunts their journeys, these characters are taken out of the safe places of conventional behaviour and belief, to the farthest reaches of themselves, both the heart of darkness and the quest for a larger meaning. In almost all cases the encounter involves a confrontation with death and the spiritual. In the title story, a man, his gay lover and his wife are drawn into a 'strange' alliance as they struggle to deal with his impending death from AIDS. 'Say' and 'Nocturne in Blue' recount the story of a rape and its retribution from the point of view of the rapist, his victim, and her healer, in a competition of narratives leading to a shocking dénouement. In 'For Ishmael' the lines in the palms of a man's hands keep changing without explanation, as he becomes embroiled in the lives and stories of others. Characters cross over into each other's stories in uncanny networks of meeting orchestrated by a dark angel who also bears witness to these tales and the nature of stories as a form of haunting.

All Peepal Tree titles are available from the website
www.peepaltreepress.com
with a money back guarantee, secure credit card
ordering and fast delivery throughout the world
at cost or less.

E-mail: contact@peepaltreepress.com